MISSING AND MURDERED CHILDREN

MISSING
AND MURDERED
CHILDREN

By Margaret O. Hyde

An Impact Book

Franklin Watts
A Division of Grolier Publishing
New York / London / Hong Kong / Sydney
Danbury, Connecticut

FRONTISPIECE:
EVERY YEAR, MORE THAN 450,000 CHILDREN RUN AWAY;
ANOTHER 127,000 ARE THROWN AWAY. MANY OF THESE
END UP LIVING ON THE STREETS.

The material listed below is reprinted with permission of the National Center for Missing and Exploited Children (NCMEC).
"My 8 Rules for Safety." Copyright © 1990 NCMEC. All rights reserved. (p. 13)
"Rules for Online Safety," adapted from *Child Safety on the Information Highway* by Lawrence J. Magid. Copyright © 1994 NCMEC. All rights reserved. (p.14)
"Common Tricks," from *KIDS AND COMPANY: TOGETHER FOR SAFETY*™. Copyright © 1988 NCMEC. All rights reserved. (p.15)
The sample flier from *Missing and Abducted Children: A Law Enforcement Guide to Case Investigation and Program Management*. Copyright © 1994 NCMEC. All rights reserved. (p. 108)

Visit Franklin Watts on the Internet at:
http//publishing.grolier.com

Photographs ©: Advertising Council, Inc.: 79, 81; AP/Wide World Photos: 18; Children of the Night: 40, 56 (Benat Doppagne); Covenant House: 36, 38; Gamma-Liaison: 30 (Frank Spooner), 77; Magnum Photos: 67 (James Nachtwey); Mark Lewis: 2; National Center for Missing and Exploited Children: 13, 24, 47; Reuters/Archive Photos: 53, 85 (Win McNamee); UPI/Corbis-Bettmann: 21.

Library of Congress Cataloging-in-Publication Data

Hyde, Margaret O. (Margaret Oldroyd)
    Missing and murdered children / by Margaret O. Hyde.
        p.   cm.—(An impact book)
    Includes bibliographical references and index.
    Summary: Discusses missing and abducted children, abused children, and murder victims, and outlines ways to prevent and cope with these increasing problems.
    ISBN 0-531-11384-1
    1. Runaway children—United States—Juvenile literature. 2. Missing children—United States—Juvenile literature. 3. Murder victims—United States—Juvenile literature. 4. Child sexual abuse—United States—Prevention—Juvenile literature. 5. Abduction—United States—Prevention—Juvenile literature. 6. Kidnapping, Parental—United States—Prevention—Juvenile literature. [1.Runaways. 2. Missing children. 3. Child abuse. 4. Murder.] I.Title
HV741.H87   1998   97-23355
                                                                 CIP   AC

CONTENTS

ONE

MISSING AND MURDERED CHILDREN

EVERY YEAR, AS MANY AS A MILLION CHILDREN MAY BE missing—away for a few hours, a few days, or even as long as forever. Some are kidnapped by strangers, or more often by parents warring over custody. Some are runaways, fleeing abuse, cruelty, or poverty, or seeking freer horizons. Some are thrownaways, tossed out like refuse by addicted, disturbed, or overwhelmed parents. And some are murdered, victims of society's problems.

Most kidnapping is by a parent who has lost custody of a child. After a divorce or legal separation, one parent is usually named as the custodial parent with responsibility for the child or the children. The noncustodial parent may have some rights, such as visitation, but this parent lacks authority. A noncustodial parent, who feels that the arrangements are unfair, sometimes becomes so angry that he or she will attempt to kidnap the child or the children.

Kidnapping by strangers is far less common than kidnapping by a parent who does not have custody of the child, but it is not uncommon. About three hundred children are gone for long periods of time or are murdered each year.[1] About five thousand kidnappings by a family member are reported to authorities each year.[2] The custodial parents left behind search for their children in every possible way. Such searches may go on for many years, for some children disappear without a trace.

Children join the ranks of the missing for other reasons, too. Every year, over half a million children are thrown away by their parents or caregivers, or run away in the hope of finding a better life.[3] Many come home in a few hours, a few days, a few years; but some never return. The thrownaways and runaways often spend years on the streets, selling their bodies to survive. Many older children try to escape their violent homes by running away, but the very young are trapped.

Among the missing and murdered children are the babies who are snatched from their carriages and cribs by women who are desperate for children of their own; those who are stolen from their parents and sold for adoption with false papers claiming that their natural mothers are dead; and the infants who are abandoned on doorsteps, in dumpsters, and on subways, some of whom are rescued and some of whom meet an early death.

The disappearances of many children go unnoticed by the public, but the occasional case is taken up by the national media. In 1996, two young parents who disposed of their newborn in a dumpster created a sensation. A six-year-old boy who dumps his neighbor's infant out of a bassinet, abusers who abduct, rape, and kill young girls or boys—these cases shock a nation into caring, at least for a short time. But the baby Jane Doe who is abandoned in the woods or the child whose young, abusive mother convinces authorities that her baby died of natural causes may go unnoticed.

The FBI (Federal Bureau of Investigation) estimates that 85 to 90 percent of all missing person reports involve juveniles.[4] While there are many groups organized (see pages 98 to 107) to prevent abductions and help families whose children are missing, young people, ranging in age from infants to teens, continue to disappear. Many of them die violent deaths.

The increasing number of young psychopaths (people without conscience) and the continuing drug scene appear to be responsible for many tragedies, especially those in which kids kill kids. The population of teens is expected to grow in the coming years and increase the violent crime rate that has been showing some signs of decreasing.

Here is a quote from the preamble to the 1981 National Symposium on Exploited and Victimized Children.

Across the nation, children are being sexually assaulted, murdered, forgotten. Some are as young as six weeks, others are three, or eight, or fifteen.

> Unfortunately, the press, law enforcement officials, politicians and the general public are unaware of just how common the problem is in every part of the country, and many children die singly and obscurely, their silent deaths lost to the American conscience.
>
> Sometimes the murders occur in groups. Periodically, reports splash across the front pages in groups of 20 and 30. But for the most part, they die alone in the backwoods and the back bedrooms of America.[5]

Sadly, these statements remain accurate descriptions of today's world.

No matter what the reason behind the disappearance of a baby, a young boy or girl, or a teen, the headline "Missing Child" strikes fear in the hearts of readers. The words usually call to mind a picture of a small, frightened child held captive in a barren room or hidden in the woods. The idea of a child being abducted, and perhaps sexually assaulted or murdered, can mobilize a community.

A few well-publicized and terrible tragedies in the 1970s and 1980s alerted the nation to the horrors of the abduction of children by strangers. By the 1990s, the cruel realization that parents and caregivers may kill their own children began to set in. Such behavior may still be difficult for most people to acknowledge, but in its first report in 1990, the U.S. Advisory Board on Child Abuse and Neglect concluded that the problem of child maltreatment and fatal abuse had escalated to the level of a national emergency. The board dedicated its 1995 report, *A Nation's Shame: Fatal Child Abuse and Neglect in the United States*, to the thousands of children who had died at the hands of parents and caregivers over a period of about two years.[6]

Tales of fatal child abuse evoke anger and revulsion in those that hear them. They may seem harder to believe than the cases of stranger kidnapping, but every year in America about two thousand children are shaken, beaten, stabbed, or pushed to their death by their own parents or caregivers.[7] Many of these children are victims of incest.

In addition to the serious problem of child abuse and neglect, there has been an increase in deaths of children from other kinds of violence. The number of deaths from nonaccidental injury rose by 47 percent from 1978 to 1991.[8]

Whether from violence connected with abductions, gang-related activities, arguments, drugs, robberies, neglect, sexual or physical abuse, children are still dying.

Two

KIDNAPPING BY STRANGERS

Is America experiencing an epidemic of kidnapping? Newspaper headlines and television news make everyone aware of the horror of kidnapping.

The Extent of Stranger Kidnapping

Many abductions and attempted abductions are not recorded. The number of reported nonfamily abductions in the United States ranges from 3,200 to 4,600 a year.[1] The majority are believed to be sexually motivated. In Canada, stranger abductions constituted less than 1 percent of all cases of missing children reported to police in 1994.[2]

Each year in the United States, there are about two hundred to three hundred cases of kidnappings in which a child is gone overnight, killed, or transported a distance of fifty miles or more.[3] In more than a fifth of the stranger abductions reported to the National Center for Missing and Exploited Children, the victims are later found dead.[4] This smaller-than-expected number of abductions does not mean that the public's concern about stranger abduction of

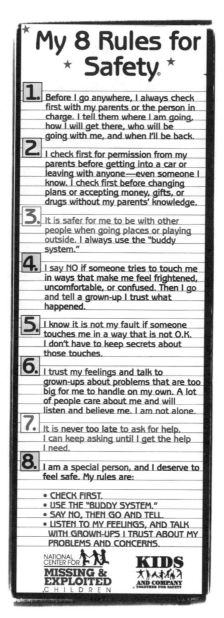

My 8 Rules for ★ Safety.

1. Before I go anywhere, I always check first with my parents or the person in charge. I tell them where I am going, how I will get there, who will be going with me, and when I'll be back.

2. I check first for permission from my parents before getting into a car or leaving with anyone—even someone I know. I check first before changing plans or accepting money, gifts, or drugs without my parents' knowledge.

3. It is safer for me to be with other people when going places or playing outside. I always use the "buddy system."

4. I say NO if someone tries to touch me in ways that make me feel frightened, uncomfortable, or confused. Then I go and tell a grown-up I trust what happened.

5. I know it is not my fault if someone touches me in a way that is not O.K. I don't have to keep secrets about those touches.

6. I trust my feelings and talk to grown-ups about problems that are too big for me to handle on my own. A lot of people care about me and will listen and believe me. I am not alone.

7. It is never too late to ask for help. I can keep asking until I get the help I need.

8. I am a special person, and I deserve to feel safe. My rules are:

- CHECK FIRST.
- USE THE "BUDDY SYSTEM."
- SAY NO, THEN GO AND TELL.
- LISTEN TO MY FEELINGS, AND TALK WITH GROWN-UPS I TRUST ABOUT MY PROBLEMS AND CONCERNS.

NATIONAL CENTER FOR **MISSING & EXPLOITED** CHILDREN

KIDS AND COMPANY • TOGETHER FOR SAFETY

THE NATIONAL CENTER FOR MISSING AND EXPLOITED CHILDREN DISTRIBUTES THIS POSTER AS PART OF A SAFETY CURRICULUM FOR ELEMENTARY SCHOOL CHILDREN.

children is unwarranted. It does mean that while children need not be constantly afraid, they should be careful.

Although it makes sense to teach children not to go with a stranger under any circumstances, they should also know that most people are not trying to snatch them away from their families. Kidnappers often attempt to lure a young child into a car or van. Teaching children to recognize the tricks that potential abductors commonly use may help them to protect themselves (see "Common Tricks," pages 16–17).

A GUIDE TO ONLINE SAFETY

- Do not give out personal information such as address, phone number, parents' work address and phone number, name and location of school without parents' permission.

- Tell your parents if you come across information that makes you uncomfortable.

- Don't agree to get together with someone you "meet" online without checking with your parents. If they agree to a meeting, make sure it is in a public place and bring along a parent.

- Don't send anyone your picture or anything else without checking with your parents.

- Don't respond to messages that are mean or make you feel uncomfortable. It is not your fault if you get messages like that. Tell your parents about it so they can contact the online service.

- Work out rules with your parents about when and how long you can be online, and which areas you can visit. Respect these rules.

Source: National Center for Missing and Exploited Children

Most teens who use the Internet have become aware of many media reports of individuals who misrepresent themselves on the information highway to lure kids to meetings. Teens need to know not to give personal information to anyone while online. Brian, who describes himself as a fourteen-year-old on the Internet, may turn out to be a thirty-year-old pedophile.

Many teens think it is harmless to make friends with others who hang around record, jewelry, or sporting goods stores in shopping malls, or at recreational events, and other places young people gather. Teens from small towns, suburbs, and cities may be unaware that these friendly people are sometimes pimps and pornographers. Teens may believe a recruiter is an exciting entrepreneur, promising a modeling or Hollywood career, a good education, a chance to win the lottery, or some other fantasy.

Although many teens are certain they can take care of themselves and are aware of the risks of "taking candy from a stranger," men and women who supply prostitutes and models for porn movies can use very clever techniques, making their offers sound enticing even to kids who are not generally considered at risk for abduction.

KIDNAPPING—AN AGE-OLD CRIME

Children have probably been stolen from their families since the days before recorded history. The word *kidnap* is a combination of *kid*, meaning "the young of a species," plus *nap*, meaning "to seize." Kidnapping was once defined as carrying someone away against that person's will and holding him or her for ransom.[5] The ransom might consist of money, political concessions, or other demands. The kidnapping of adults for ransom has become a multimillion-dollar criminal industry in some countries of Latin America, where guerrillas, ex-guerrillas, drug gangs, and common criminals all get into the act.[6]

COMMON TRICKS

The Offer Trick

The child is offered something he or she might want. The person might offer candy, a toy, gum, money, food, a ride, or a trip. Sometimes a person will take something that belongs to the child and then offer to give it back if the child goes with the person or keeps a "touching secret."

The Animal Trick

The child is attracted by a puppy or kitten or some other cute or unusual animal. The child might be tempted to go with the person or to keep a "touching secret" in order to see or play with the animal.

The Emergency Trick

The person pretends that a fire, accident, illness, death, or other emergency has happened to the child's family or home. The person offers to take the child home or to the parents.

The Help Trick

Someone older asks a child for help. The person might ask directions; ask to use the phone; or ask help looking for a lost pet, a lost child, or lost money. The person might ask for help opening a door or carrying something.

The Friend Trick

A person pretends to know the child's parents and says they have asked him or her to come and get the child.

The Bad Child Trick

A person accuses the child of doing something wrong. The child is told he or she must go with the person. The person may show the child a fake police or security guard badge. Sometimes, a person tells the child that the parents do not want him or her anymore because the child is so bad.

The Flattery Trick

The person might ask the child to go with him or her and have pictures taken. Videotaping may also be used as an excuse.

The Open the Door Trick

The person tricks the child into opening the door to his or her house when the parents are not home. The person might look like a repair person, or need to use the phone, or deliver a package.

The Secret Trick

Sometimes, children are tricked into keeping "touching secrets" because they have been told no one will believe them, that they are to blame, that their parents will be really angry, or that something bad will happen to them or their parents if they tell.

Source: National Center for Missing and Exploited Children

REASONS FOR STRANGER KIDNAPPING

On relatively rare occasions, children are abducted for ransom. An epidemic of abductions of children for ransom in Mexico recently caused much alarm in that country, especially since some of the cases appeared to involve local police.[7]

Children were, and still are, stolen by strangers for a number of reasons other than ransom, such as sexual gratification, to prevent their testimony in court, for sale to a sexual abuse ring, and as acts of war.

Hundreds of children are believed to have been kidnapped by the military during the civil war in El Salvador (1979–1992). They were taken in attacks on peasant settle-

IN SAN SALVADOR, MOTHERS OF CHILDREN WHO
DISAPPEARED DURING THE BITTER CIVIL WAR
PERIOD DEMONSTRATE TO DEMAND INFORMATION
ABOUT THE MISSING.

ments to punish the people for harboring guerrilla fighters
or sympathizing with the leftist insurgency. Some of these
children were reunited with their parents in 1996, but others are still missing.[8]

A rare reason for kidnapping children is in order to kill
them. Such was apparently the case in Atlanta in the early
1980s, when twenty-nine young black males ages seven to
twenty-seven were abducted and killed by a disturbed person in an act of racial hatred.[9]

ABDUCTION OF INFANTS

The taking of infants by a nonfamily member is not a crime of epidemic proportions, but it draws a great deal of public attention because of the vulnerability of the victims. Most cases of infant abduction take place in hospital nurseries, homes, cars, and shopping centers. In a typical hospital abduction, for example, the unknown abductor impersonates a nurse, hospital employee, volunteer, or relative in order to gain access to the infant.[10]

The motive often appears to be the kidnapper's need to fill a void in his or her life. Suppose a young mother loses her baby to cancer when the infant is six months old. She feels that she will never be happy until she has another child, but she is afraid that that child, too, might develop cancer. Her husband and her doctor assure her that this is very unlikely, but she is so confused by her loss that she cannot think clearly.

Day after day, the bereaved mother walks around shopping centers, looking longingly at babies in their strollers. When she sees an unattended baby, she is overcome by her need to have a child of her own. She snatches the infant and walks away through the crowd. When she reaches home, she tells her husband that someone gave her the baby to adopt. Sensing the truth, he calls 911, and the baby is soon returned to the mother. Not all babies are returned this quickly. In some cases, abductions remain unsolved or have tragic endings.

Even when children are carefully watched, they can be victims of abduction. In the summer of 1996, television programs in Rochester, New York, were interrupted by the announcement that a young man had just confessed to killing Kali Ann Poulton two years earlier and had told police where to find her body. Kali, who was four years old when she was stolen, vanished from the walk in front of her home even though her mother was checking on her periodically through a window. The kidnapper in this case was not a stranger; he was a neighbor.[11] During the two years in which Kali was missing, numerous posters displaying her picture and a song, "Have You Seen Kali?," enlisted thousands of people in the search for the child.

The Lindbergh Kidnapping

A kidnapping that occurred in 1932 still generates interest. The case involved Charles Lindbergh, who was the first flier to cross the Atlantic Ocean alone. Lindbergh's fame may have played a part in the sad story of the abduction of his baby.

From the time that it was discovered that the boy was missing from his crib, large numbers of Americans were transfixed by the case. A house painter was eventually executed for the crime of murdering the child, but to this day, there are people who believe he was innocent.

The Emotional Impact of Kidnapping

The panic and helplessness that follows the realization that a child may have been stolen is overwhelming. After learning of such tragedies, many parents react with fear for their own children's safety.

The fear of kidnapping by strangers is so great that rumors and imaginary stories may quickly spread through a community. One such story took on major proportions, but had no basis in truth. It told of a family visiting Disney World who claimed that their toddler was stolen when they glanced away for a couple of minutes. The mother reported the kidnapping to the security office and the gates to the park were immediately shut. The story became more elaborate and detailed as it spread. The parents were said to

THE KIDNAPPING OF THE LINDBERGH BABY IN 1932
LED TO A NATIONWIDE SEARCH FOR THE CHILD AND,
ULTIMATELY, PASSAGE OF THE FEDERAL KIDNAPPING ACT.

have been taken to a video room where they could watch all the visitors slowly being allowed to exit the park. They saw a small boy asleep in a woman's arms, and he was wearing their child's clothing. It was the stolen toddler. Out of this story, rumors spread that two hundred children were stolen each year at Disney World. However, police records show that there has never been a kidnapping reported at Disney World.[12]

Abduction Locations

Some children are taken by force, as in the case of Kristina Jacobson of Salem, Oregon. This seven-year-old was kidnapped from her babysitter's home. The abductor barged inside when the sitter answered the door, claiming that he was looking for a dog. He grabbed Kristina and took her for a one-hundred-mile ride before he was killed by a police sharpshooter.[13]

Now and then, a baby is inadvertently abducted when a car is stolen. About 8 P.M. one Thursday night, Tiffany Winfield left her car with the motor running to pick up her dinner at a fast-food outlet. When she returned, the car, with two men in it, was backing away. The thieves probably did not realize that an eleven-month-old baby was sleeping in an infant seat in the back of the car.

Over the next sixteen hours, police officers and federal agents searched for the missing car. During the long night, the mother and her family prayed that the baby would be safely returned. The next day, a young woman saw a strange car parked in her neighborhood, seventy-five miles away from the Winfield home. When she looked inside, she saw a baby. Excitedly, she called a neighbor, who in turn called the police. Winfield's address and phone number were found in the car, and she was notified. At first, she was afraid to believe that her baby had been found. The car thieves had evidently fed the infant, and she was in good health. The mother's irresponsible behavior in leaving her infant alone in an unlocked car with the motor running had put the child at great risk but had not, this time, ended in tragedy.[14]

A Spotlight on Kidnapping

As national news coverage has increased, the public has become more aware of the problem of kidnapping. Etan Patz was one of the first missing children to become famous through media coverage. In 1979, this six-year-old boy kissed his mother good-bye and started a one-and-a-half-block walk from his home to the corner where he would wait for the school bus that would take him to his first-grade class at Public School 3 in New York City. It was the first morning that he walked to the bus stop alone—and it was the last. Etan never boarded his bus. He disappeared and has never been found, even though the search for him has been extensive and the mass media was mobilized in the efforts to find this missing child.[15]

The case of the disappearance of Adam Walsh sent

Missing: 05/25/79	Age Now: 24 Yr
Missing From: NEW YORK, NY	
Birth: 10/09/72	Age Disap.: 6 Yr
Sex: M	Race: WHITE
Height: 3'4"	Weight: 50 lbs
Hair: L BROWN	Eyes: BLUE

Id Info: Child was wearing black cap, blue corduroy jacket, blue pants, blue sneakers and carrying a blue bag with elephants on it.

Circum: Last seen at 8:00 a.m. at Prince St. and Wooster St. going to the school bus stop.

ANYONE HAVING INFORMATION SHOULD CONTACT
The National Center for Missing and Exploited Children
1-800-843-5678
OR

NEW YORK POLICE DEPARTMENT (NEW YORK) —
MISSING PERSONS UNIT — 1-212-233-4152

NEARLY TWENTY YEARS AFTER HE DISAPPEARED FROM A MAN-
HATTAN STREET, THE SEARCH FOR ETAN PATZ CONTINUES.

chills through the nation. On July 27, 1981, this six-year-old boy waited in the toy department of a Florida store while his mother looked at lamps nearby. A few minutes after she had left him, Adam disappeared. His mother had him paged both in the store and out in the mall. There was no response. The police were called, and the parents assured them that Adam would not wander off by himself. His photograph and a full description were given to police and local television stations. Numerous posters made his face familiar to thousands of people. Volunteers searched the neighborhood. The local police notified other departments in the state. But by the next morning, Adam had not been found. About two weeks later, the remains of Adam's body were discovered in a ditch about a hundred miles from his home. The case was never solved.[16]

Ten-year-old Kevin Collins was another famous missing child. He disappeared on February 10, 1984, in San Francisco, California, after attending basketball practice. He was last seen at a bus stop near his school, and in spite of a massive search, he has never been found.[17]

Stories of children being kidnapped and sacrificed in satanic rituals or of babies being sold to childless couples from other countries were common in the 1980s. Even today, one hears of parents in Mexico and Guatemala who fear that their children are being kidnapped and smuggled into the United States where their body parts are sold to rich Americans who need organ transplants.[18] While most of these horror stories are nothing more than fantasies, they have played a role in alerting the public to the problem of missing children.

The Missing Children Movement

Well-publicized cases like those of Etan Patz, Adam Walsh, and Kevin Collins led to the growth of a movement to increase public awareness of missing children. Large numbers of people joined together in efforts to fight stranger abduction. Children were fingerprinted and the prints put on file. Parents warned their children about talking to strangers so emphatically that many were afraid even to respond to a salesperson's casual questions. Exaggerated reports surfaced, with estimates of 1.5 million children stolen and thousands disappearing without a trace across the United States each year.

Certainly, one missing child is one too many, but the intense media coverage of a few cases made stranger abduction seem like an ever-present menace. This conception grew, leading the way to legislation aimed at improving efforts to search for children who were missing for any reason.

THREE

PARENTAL CHILD SNATCHING

POSTERS; PICTURES ON TELEPHONE POLES, TREES, shopping bags, and government bulletin boards; and postcards often carry messages about missing children. Many of these are children who have been abducted by a parent. In fact, the majority of children reported missing have been stolen by parents who do not have legal custody.

Advo, Inc., the nation's largest direct mail corporation, has been sending out millions of advertisements each week for the past dozen years with pictures of missing children on the address side of the card. Their "Have You Seen Me?" ads include a picture and descriptive information about each child and request that anyone who recognizes a child call 1-800-THE-LOST, the number for the National Center for Missing and Exploited Children. Most of the children found through the Advo cards were abducted by one of their parents.[1]

A TYPICAL CASE

Mary's story might be a typical case. A postcard with pictures of this five-year-old girl and her mother shocked the

Lang family when it arrived in the mail. They had received similar cards with pictures of missing children from time to time, but this card, running an ad for automotive services on the other side, carried the faces of their neighbors.

The child, who was described as having been missing for more than a year, was named Maribel. Information under her mother's picture revealed that she had abducted her daughter from the child's father, who had been awarded legal custody. The name the woman now used was listed as an alias. The child's name had been changed from Maribel to Mary, the name by which the Langs knew her.

The Langs were troubled. Should they call the police? Should they warn Mary's mother that other people in the neighborhood would probably recognize her and call the police? Before they had made a decision, Mary's mother, having learned about the postcards, had packed as much as she could fit into her van and whisked Mary away. She did not say good-bye to anyone, she did not leave an address, and she has never been heard from again.

REUNION AFTER A LONG ABSENCE

Some children who are abducted by a parent or other family member are never found. Some are found only after many years have passed. Such was the case with Leonard Joseph Cammalleri, who was abducted by his father at the age of ten months and was not reunited with his mother until 1996, when he was thirteen years old. His mother was happy but overwhelmed by the sight of her son, now an adolescent. She remembered him as a baby in diapers, weighing twenty-five pounds. Now he was a thin, frail teenager.

Until Leonard's reunion with his mother, his life had been much like that of other children who have been abducted by a noncustodial parent. His father had told him that his mother or the police might break down the door of their home at any time. He was not allowed to go to school or have playmates. Instead, his father taught him at home, read to him, and took him to the park from time to time. He grew up knowing that he and his father were "wanted," so they had to hide.[2] Photographs of both Leonard and Mr. Cammalleri appeared on leaflets distributed by the National Center for Missing and Exploited Children, and father and son were the subject of a nationwide search involving the Federal Bureau of Investigation.

LIFE ON THE RUN

Authorities tell of instances of parental abduction in which children have been tied to furniture, kept from school and medical attention, and had their hair dyed and appearances changed so that they would not be recognized. In the case of Autumn Young, five years passed from the time that her mother told her father that he would never see his daughter again. During those five years, Autumn's father spent his savings on lawyers and detectives who searched for her. When he finally found her in Florida, her eyebrows were encrusted with dirt, her clothes were torn, and her skin was a ghostly white because she had been kept hidden inside the house. Her father was given custody, and she started a new and good life with him and his new wife.[3]

Some children who are abducted by a parent do attend school, but they may move often, having their names changed each time to prevent discovery. The fact that a child has changed schools frequently may alert school officials to the possibility of abduction or other problems in the child's history.

Imagine the life of a child who must remember to use a new name, make new friends, and live "on the run." Leaving new friends and possessions behind, lying about the past, and living in fear of being discovered make life very difficult. Worrying about the parent left behind can be a serious emotional problem for the child.

Often the abducting parents tell their children that the parents they left behind died or did not love them anymore. In most cases, these are lies, and the parents from whom these children have been taken search for them in every possible way.

REASONS FOR PARENTAL ABDUCTION

Reasons for parental abduction vary. A child snatcher is frequently desperate and perceives abduction as the only way to right a wrong. A confused parent, unable to accept a separation or divorce, may feel that stealing the child will make the custodial parent want him or her back in order to regain the child. Some noncustodial parents are willing to make any sacrifice to hold on to their children.

One common reason for parental kidnapping is a wish to get back at a hated spouse. About half of the abductors in a study reported in *When Parents Kidnap* had been violent toward their spouse during the marriage. Such spousal abuse must have been upsetting to the child during the marriage and may add to the fears of a child living with the violent parent. Almost half of parental kidnappers threatened that an abduction was going to occur, and one in seven used force to carry it out.[4]

In general, abductors had records of tendencies toward violence in their marriages. They were seen to have close relationships with their children, but not as close as those of the custodial parents.[5]

A noncustodial parent may feel that a court decision at a divorce is unfair. Or that parent may believe that the custodial parent has an alcohol or a drug problem or is sexually abusive or violent, promiscuous, or unfit for some other reason, and the child must be removed for his or her own safety.

One of the most famous cases in which a parent claimed that the motive for abduction was to protect the

WANTED FOR CHILD ABDUCTION

BERNARD DOWNES (natural father) snatched his daughter Vida Fenton, aged 2, from her mother's home in Hornsey, London on Friday 5th July.
Downes, 28, is white, of Anglo-Asian appearance, slim build, 5'-9" tall, with straight, short-cropped hair and brown eyes. He may be disguised. He has boyish looks and speaks with a nasal droning voice and a Lancashire accent.

If seen DO NOT APPROACH but contact
the local police station or

HIGHBURY VALE POLICE STATION
211 Blackstock Road, London, N5

TEL: 071•263 9090

PARENTAL ABDUCTIONS ARE A GROWING PROBLEM
THROUGHOUT THE WORLD.

child is that of Hilary Morgan, the daughter of Elizabeth Morgan, a physician, and Eric Foretich, a dental surgeon. The legal battle began when Hilary was less than seven months old and continued for seven more years. Dr. Morgan, who had legal custody, hid Hilary to prevent her father from taking her for overnight visits because she believed he was sexually abusing the child. Dr. Morgan spent twenty-five months in jail rather than reveal the whereabouts of her daughter. During this time, Hilary was in hiding with her grandparents in Canada, Great Britain, and New Zealand. When Dr. Morgan was released from jail, she went to New Zealand to be with her daughter. In 1996, when Hilary was fourteen, Congress passed a bill allowing both mother and daughter to return to the United States without legal repercussions. The girl's father vowed to fight this legislation.[6]

COPING WITH ABDUCTION

Children who have been abducted cope with their situation in a variety of ways. Some, like Tammy, learn to mask their feelings as a means of protection. Tammy seemed well adjusted to life with her father, who had abducted her one afternoon as she was walking home from school. She enjoyed the new clothing he bought for her, the movies her mother would never allow her see, and many other privileges. She never mentioned how much she missed her mother, but every night she cried herself to sleep.

Many children continue to love the parents who have abducted them and see them as rescuers. This is often a way of muffling the pain at the loss of the parent who is left behind, but in some cases, children are really glad to have been rescued from a bad situation.

The effect of abduction on children varies greatly. Not all children are irreparably damaged by the experience, and positive relationships and nurturing can help children who have experienced great stress.[7] However, most abducted children suffer in many ways. Parental abduction is often heartbreaking. Common reactions among the victims include fear, worry, and frequent crying. Some of the responses to parental abduction, such as fear and nightmares, are similar to effects noted in other kidnap victims.[8] They may be long lasting as well, even affecting the victim's own parenting.

The age of the abducted child is an important factor in determining how that child will be affected by being cut off from one parent. Very young children may be aware that something is wrong and may feel responsible for the parents' anger. They may feel like bad children experiencing their own anger—at their parents and the situation—and may then act like bad children until it is a way of life.

Concerns about losing a parent and preoccupation with death are especially acute in abducted five- to six-year-olds. At this age, children are aware of time and know how long they have been "on the run." In school, they know they are different from their classmates, and they feel guilty about lying about family names and backgrounds.

Most cases of parental abduction involve children younger than nine years of age.[9] For these children, and even for older children who are still in the process of establishing their own identity, lying to authorities interferes with normal development.[10]

While some younger children make a game of hiding, others try to call home. Adolescents may be willing accomplices in their abduction, secretly helping to arrange to escape from home without causing suspicion. But these children may still suffer from loyalty conflicts as they wonder what is happening to the parent they left behind. Older children may blame themselves for not contacting the searching parent—a feeling that may continue even after a reunion.[11] And they may wrestle with feelings of guilt, fear, loyalty, love, and shame while living under cover and in the following years.

PARENTAL KIDNAPPING LAWS

Children who are abducted by a parent are clearly at risk of emotional trauma and neglect. All fifty states and the District of Columbia have now enacted civil and criminal laws that apply to parental kidnapping cases.[12] Under the Parental Kidnapping Prevention Act of 1980, the home state is given priority for jurisdiction. The FBI can enter the search for children who have been taken across state lines or out of the country.

Connie's husband kidnapped their children ten years ago and took them to his native country, Iran. She made every possible effort to find them, but she has finally given up hope of ever seeing them again. A number of countries participate in the Hague Convention on the Civil Aspects of International Child Abduction, but Iran is not one of them. This treaty, which the United States ratified in 1988, provides that, subject to certain exceptions, a child who has been taken unlawfully from a ratifying country should be returned to his or her home country.[13]

An estimated five to six hundred children a year are taken or detained in international child abductions.[14] If a parent believes that a child may have been taken to a foreign country, he or she may contact the National Center for Missing and Exploited Children at 703-235-3900, or 1-800-THE LOST to discuss the filing of an application invoking the Hague Convention. The Hague Convention has improved the likelihood and speed of return of abducted and wrongfully detained children from the forty-five countries that are party to the agreement.

Hundreds of thousands of parents have not recovered children who were abducted to other states or countries, and they are continuing their searches. The National Center for Missing and Exploited Children and the U.S. Department of State may work on more than a thousand cases in a single year. Many parents live in continuous pain while they search and wait.[15]

Almost all cases of parental abduction involve a tremendous amount of suffering on the part of the parents, children, and extended families.

FOUR

RUNAWAYS, THROWNAWAYS, AND OTHER MISSING CHILDREN

TARA, WHOSE STEPFATHER SEXUALLY ABUSED HER FOR three years, ran away from home when she was fifteen to try to find a better life.

Sixteen-year-old Matt could not persuade his father to let him buy his own car. He had money saved from part-time jobs, but his father insisted that it was not enough to buy a safe car. When Matt threatened to run away, his father told him to do what he pleased. So he went to California with a friend, where he planned to buy a car and start a new life.

Larry, an overprotected, adopted twelve-year-old, ran away to try to find his natural mother. He believed she had to be better than the one who nagged all the time.

No matter what the reason, running away from home is more dangerous now than it was in the past, even though it was not always safe then, either. Running away has a place in America's folklore, but the reality is far different from the fictional experiences of Tom Sawyer and Huckleberry Finn. The mischievous children of folklore, adventurous boys and girls who ran off to see the world, have little in common with today's runaways.

RUNNING FROM TROUBLE TO TROUBLE

The main reason children or teenagers run away today is to escape from long and painful family conflicts or from physical, sexual, or psychological abuse.[1]

Many runaways leave home with a little money, usually just enough to get to a big city where they believe they will be able to find work. If they don't find jobs soon after they arrive, they cannot afford a place to live. Sarah tried to get a job, but she could not deal with the hard work and long hours waiting on tables in a greasy diner, the only place she managed to get work without proof that she was old enough to be hired. After two days, she quit and joined some street-smart kids who lived as a family in a crash pad. They lived by a rigid code that applied to everyone in the group. In addition to free love at the pad, Sarah was forced to earn money by having sex with strangers. She stole food and became involved in drug dealing so that she would be accepted by the family. She endured endless hours of waiting for customers, living in filth, and squabbling.

After a few months, Sarah looked for alternatives to living with the group. One of her options was to call a runaway hotline number which was posted in a store window, in order to find a local shelter. She might get in the gray van that cruised the streets each night taking kids to Covenant House Another option was to go home, but anything seemed better than dealing with the abuse from her mother's live-in boyfriend. Still, Sarah was worried that she might have been infected with HIV by one of her customers. She knew she had to do something to get away from where she was living and find a better life.

Sarah never even had the money to make a phone call, an arrangement that helped to keep kids in the group. When she saw a poster with directions for calling Covenant House by dialing the operator and asking for the 1-800 hotline at Covenant House, she made the call. Covenant House has shelters in a number of cities in the United

THE COVENANT HOUSE VAN OFFERS A RIDE BACK FROM LIFE ON THE STREETS.

States and one in Canada. Each caller is helped by a counselor who discusses his or her situation. In some cases, as in Sarah's, arrangements are made for health care. Sarah was offered a test for HIV and a place at a shelter. She learned that her HIV test was negative and had a number of sessions with another counselor. Together they made plans for Sarah to live in a city-run halfway house and return to public school.

Runaways are the least publicized of all missing children,[2] however, they are the most numerous.[3] Most runaways are teenagers, and they tend to come from households with a stepparent and with long-term problems of physical and emotional abuse.[4] Alcohol and other drug abuse and difficulties with school staff, friends, or police are common reasons for leaving home. Many children run away from home and juvenile facilities time after time.

Estimates of the total number of runaways per year vary, but the National Center for Missing and Exploited Children states the figure may be about 500,000. About half of them are back home by bedtime. One in ten travel a distance of more than one hundred miles while gone.[5] Long-term runaways are at greatest risk of resorting to prostitution, suffering from medical problems, and becoming victims of violence.[6]

THROWNAWAYS

Thrownaways are kids who are forced out of their homes for a variety of reasons. The word *throwaway*, which is sometimes used to describe these children, implies that the children are useless and disposable, while *thrownaways* conveys a more accurate picture of what has been done to them.[7]

In some cases, children are thrown away because they are seen as intolerable financial burdens by the parents. Or they are in the way of parents who do not want children. In many cases, parents no longer want to, or feel able to, deal with a child who is troublesome. Syd, for example, was arrested a number of times. Each time he returned home he continued to disobey his parents' and society's rules. His parents finally told him to leave. In another instance, Martin, who was gay, came out to his family in the hope that they would accept him. His mother and sister were upset about his homosexuality, but they were understanding. This was not the case with his father, who threw him out of the house and told him never to come back. He lived on the streets, earning money by having sex with older men and panhandling.

YOUTH SHELTERS AND CRISIS CENTERS MAINTAIN TOLL-FREE, TWENTY-FOUR-HOUR HOTLINES TO OFFER HELP TO YOUNG PEOPLE IN DISTRESS.

Thrownaways are not always reported to the police as missing children. Some parents pretend to search for kids but do not really want or try to find them. Thrownaways suffer the same problems as runaways, but they generally do not have the luxury of opting to return home. Some children are allowed to come and go for weeks at a time without supervision, and they are also classed as thrownaways, even though they can return home.[8] Home may be a hateful place, but it is usually better than living on the streets.

Cruelty and neglect is found in families at every economic level and in all social groups. The incidence of thrownaways is higher in low-income families and families without both natural parents—perhaps because these families have fewer options and resources. They lack the ability to send difficult or rebellious children to boarding schools or residences, or to obtain the help of professional counselors or therapists. The parents may also be living in such conditions of poverty and hopelessness that they may be overwhelmed by despair.[9]

NEW LAWS TO PROTECT RUNAWAYS AND THROWNAWAYS

Over the years, child advocates have tried to improve the lot of runaways, thrownaways, and other missing children. The laws that created the juvenile courts at the beginning of the twentieth century also authorized the detention of runaways in local facilities and state-level training schools. Some runaways were held longer than juveniles who had committed serious criminal acts, such as robbery, rape, or homicide.[10] In many cases, this holding of runaways and thrownaways in institutions with delinquents created more problems than it solved. The institutions were "schools for criminals" where the runaways learned how to break laws and become serious delinquents themselves.[11]

Government task forces and child advocates have been successful in passing a number of acts to protect runaways and other missing children. Beginning with the passage of the Federal Kidnapping Act in 1932 (commonly called the Lindbergh Law), about a dozen different laws have been passed to help protect children from kidnapping and to find missing children.[12]

During the 1960s, Congress was presented with dramatic accounts of the ill treatment of runaway children in detention homes and adult jails. Some professionals testified that the juvenile justice system's control over runaways and many other children was counterproductive.[13] Congress responded to these charges by passing the Juvenile Justice and Delinquency Prevention Act of 1974. This act labeled runaways, school truants, and some other groups as "status offenders," that is, juveniles whose acts are considered crimes because of their youth. It stated that runaway children could not be taken into custody and held in secure places. Instead, they were to be placed in group homes and nonsecure shelters which they could leave whenever they wished, regardless of the risks they faced on the street.

The Runaway Youth Act of 1974 and later legislation enable the Department of Health and Human Services to fund some shelters and halfway houses for runaways. Most shelters provide counseling to help runaways through a crisis situation with their families, but the families may remain troubled. Government programs are not extensive enough to meet the needs of many missing children.[14]

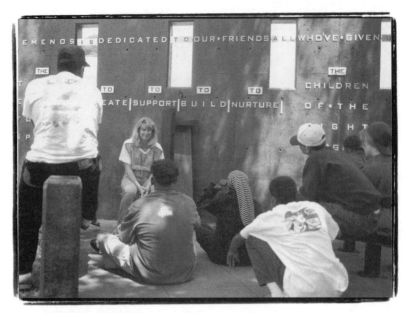

STAFF MEMBERS AND VOLUNTEERS AT YOUTH SHELTERS
AND OTHER AGENCIES ACROSS THE COUNTRY WORK TO
HELP YOUNG PEOPLE REBUILD THEIR LIVES.

The Missing Children Act of 1982 was the first piece
of legislation specifically addressing the problems of
missing children. It ensures that complete descriptions
of missing children can be entered in the Federal Bureau of
Investigation's National Crime Information Center computer, even when the abductor has not been charged with a
crime. In 1984, The Missing Children's Assistance Act
added a number of benefits for missing children, such as
the creation of the National Center for Missing and
Exploited Children (NCMEC), the operation of a twenty-
four-hour hotline, and the funding of research. In addition
to other new laws that were passed in the years that fol-
lowed, the Child Abduction Flagging Mechanism went into
effect in 1997. Now, especially suspicious or dangerous
abduction cases receive priority in the computerized infor-

mation system for Missing and Exploited Children and the FBI's Child Abduction and Serial Killer Unit.

LOST CHILDREN

Lost children have always been a serious concern for parents and communities. The "Lost, Injured, or Otherwise Missing" category in the Department of Justice report includes over 400,000 children each year. Almost half of them are under the age of four. Nearly one-fifth of them experience physical harm. About 14 percent are abused or assaulted during the episode.[15]

Many young children wander off from home or from the residence of a parent or guardian, but most are soon found by their parents or neighbors. Others become lost in the woods, in stores, in shopping centers, and other urban areas. In rare cases, children disappear because they fall into wells, pools, or large bodies of water.

The ways that children get lost vary widely. An autistic child wandered away from home and survived four days before being recovered.[16] Fourteen-year-old Melissa disappeared after she took the drug Ecstasy at a rock concert. She went home with a man who lived in another state after wandering around New York City. Her family located her after a huge search.[17] Many children wander away from campgrounds while families are on vacation, and some are lost in nearby woods.

FIVE

MY SISTER IS MISSING!
THE SEARCH

WHEN A CHILD DISAPPEARS, THE WHOLE FAMILY IS affected. The following account, based on actual cases, describes one family's experience as told by the teenage brother of the abduction victim.

The search for my sister Lisa began the day she didn't come home from soccer practice. She is only ten, but she is mature and she always calls if she is going to be late. When she was an hour late, my mother called all Lisa's friends to see if she had gone home with them. Lisa knew she would be grounded for not asking permission, but she always called to let my parents know that she was OK when she did go somewhere without asking. After a couple of hours, with no sign of Lisa, my mother called 911 to report that she was missing.

Police officers came to our house and they interviewed all of us. Then they interviewed Lisa's teacher and some of her friends to see if her actions were out of character. They told us there was high risk of foul play in Lisa's case, and an immediate full-scale response was warranted.

Since many experts believe that abducted children face the greatest danger during the first few hours after the abduction, no time was wasted in beginning the search for Lisa. A decade ago if a child ten or older disappeared, the common attitude was that he or she had just run away. Mandatory waiting periods of forty-eight to seventy-two hours were common for police departments.[1] During these hours, families were anguished, and many missing children were facing extreme danger and were sometimes killed by their abductors.

My mother cooperated with every suggestion that the police made. Afterward, she said she had been too frightened to cry during the first few days. I tried to help my mother. She was so upset that she couldn't make dinner or eat anything I made. She didn't sleep, and paced the floor for hours. The social worker who came to the house said that most missing children are either found or return home on their own within a few days, but my mother didn't seem to hear.

My mother imagined Lisa in terrible situations, trapped in some hidden place, lying injured or unconscious out of sight, or abducted by a stranger for purposes she could not describe. She later told me that she had a nightmare in which Lisa was stolen by a man who sold her to a pornography ring and then killed her because she would not cooperate.

I managed to reach my father a few hours after the police began their search. He was on a business trip, but he came home as soon as we located him. He arrived home frantic about Lisa's disappearance, and he was very angry because the police acted as if he were the one who had abducted Lisa. They said that most disappearances were runaways or parental abductions. When they believed that he was not involved, the police asked him all the questions that they had already asked us.

The police report included everything—information about what clothes and jewelry Lisa was wearing, her height, her hair and skin color and eye color. They asked if she had ever been fingerprinted and whether she had ever had surgery and had her blood typed. They took some hair from her hairbrush, because blood and hair samples could be used in identification if anything awful had happened.

In the next week, we ordered call-waiting for our phone, and call-forwarding to a cellular phone that someone in the family carried all the time. We kept a record of all calls in a notebook. A police officer stayed at our house for the first few days to listen to any phone calls that might help in the search. Every time the phone rang, we hoped it would be news about Lisa. Every morning, I hoped she would turn up that day.[2]

The police learned that one of Lisa's friends had seen a pickup truck near the soccer field the day she disappeared. Officers fanned out on the highways looking for a truck fitting the description. A volunteer group of twenty-four people searched the nearby woods with cellular phones, first-aid kits, and dogs trained to find missing people. While neighbors and other volunteers were combing the neighborhood, the National Center for Missing and Exploited Children faxed a photo of Lisa to more than six thousand law enforcement agencies throughout the nation. An electronic photo of Lisa was sent across the country by computer, along with basic information such as her birth date, hair and eye color, height, and the date she disappeared. National printshop chains converted the images into high-quality hard copies and local volunteers distributed several thousand posters to libraries, supermarkets, and transportation hubs.

The National Center for Missing and Exploited Children arranged for national media coverage of the search for Lisa through its partnership with major television networks, leading publications, and major corporations. Law enforcement officers entered her name in the FBI's Missing Persons File, and they listed her with a number of service agencies that search for missing children. They checked with runaway shelters, even though there was little reason to think she had run away, and with health care providers in case she had had an accident and could not call home. Everything possible was being done to find her. The family was encouraged by learning that the National Center for Missing and Exploited Children has played a part in the recovery of about 34,000 children since it began in 1984.[3] Perhaps they would find Lisa.

Information under the posters with Lisa's picture asked anyone who had seen her to call the twenty-four-hour toll-free hotline: 1-800-THE-LOST (1-800-843-5678). The hotline is available throughout the United States, Canada, and Mexico and operates around the clock every day of the year. About seven hundred calls are received each weekday.

Lisa's picture and the information about her was on the Missing Children Website of the National Center for Missing and Exploited Children. With the help of a computer teacher at school, we placed a link on the homepage of our computer by using this:

<A HREF="http://www.missingkids.com/">National Center for Missing and Exploited Children</a>

People visiting the website see images of many missing children. The twelve most recently reported children are kept in a queue and the image changes every ten minutes. While Lisa was in the queue her picture and information about her was seen by every computer user who visited the website of the National Center for Missing and Exploited Children.[4]

AGE-PROGRESSION IMAGING

If Lisa is not found in the next few years, computerized age-progression photos of her will be created by artists at the National Center for Missing and Exploited Children to show how she will probably look as she grows older. If these photos are circulated, the chance of finding her is better. Some remarkable likenesses of children who have been located years after their abduction have been generated through this process of age-progression drawings.[5] Glenn Miller is one of the artists at the center who knows how to blend science and art to show how a child will probably look when he or she is years older than the picture from which he works. His software program replicates children's growth patterns. For instance, faces develop dramatically until the age of seven, but the head size remains the same. Miller refers to thousands of photographs of children of various ages and ethnic backgrounds in his work. He uses childhood pictures of the parents when possible, to try to determine from the missing child's photos which features have been inherited from each parent.

Here is how he works with the photo of a girl who disappeared when she was seven and who would now be fourteen. With his computer, he removes the childish puff from her cheeks and makes her face longer. He compares her face with a picture of her older brother and gives her some of his more mature features.

The process of producing computer age-progression of a missing child's photograph:

Step 1 First, photographs are collected. These include the last-known picture of the missing child, and pictures of the biological parents and siblings at the missing child's present age. If the child was abducted at age three and would now be nine, photographs of the parents and siblings at age nine would be requested. These photographs provide the computer-age progression specialist with information about growth, family likenesses and unique features, and facial patterns influenced by heredity.

Step 2. The last-known photograph of the child before abduction is scanned into the computer.

Step 3 The child's photograph is stretched to conform to the dimensions of the photgraph of the child's nine-year-old brother.

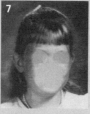

Step 4 The photo of the brother is scanned into the computer.

Step 5 The child's stretched photo (right half) is merged with that of her brother.

Step 6 The resulting merged photograph

Step 7 A photograph of a nine-year-old girl is chosen from the reference file to supply typical hairstyle and clothing and is scanned in.

Step 8 The photos are merged, to transfer hair and dress to the missing child's aged image.

Step 9 The final age-progressed image of the child as a nine-year-old

Step 10 Actual photograph of the abducted child at age nine—after her recovery.

Very young children are more difficult to age-progress than older ones.[6] Since Lisa was ten, there is hope that the age-progression artist can create an accurate picture of how she will look in the following years if she is not found quickly.

> Many people are still searching for Lisa. Every day we hope she'll be found and brought home safely. But as more time passes, we lose hope. There's a giant hole in our lives. Counselors tell us that the distress we feel is like that experienced by people who have gone through other terrible experiences—war veterans, children who've been badly burned, victims of rape, assault, and other violent crimes.[7] We will not stop searching for Lisa until she is found.

SEARCHING YESTERDAY AND TODAY

New methods of searching for missing children have greatly improved the chances of finding them. About ten years ago, a mentally retarded boy was abandoned by friends with whom he had traveled to a nearby city. They gave him money and told him to go home, but he was not capable of finding his way. He became lost and was taken to a police station. From there he was taken to a city children's center, but he could not identify himself. The boy's father alerted police in his suburban community the day his son did not return, and they conducted a search. But the boy spent eight months in the children's center before being located because the city police did not know who he was.[8] If this boy were lost today, the police in his community could report him to the FBI's National Crime Information Center's computerized Missing Persons File, and the city police could report him to the FBI's Unidentified Persons File. In this way, a match could be made quickly.[9] But even with today's technology, many searches are long, complicated, and not always successful.

RECOVERING CHILDREN FROM PARENTAL ABDUCTIONS

Most missing children are recoverable. In fact, many of those who have been abducted by parents are attending school and living openly in neighborhoods where no one is aware that they are really missing children.

When the left-behind parents search for children, they have many possible avenues to follow. For example, it is possible for police to run a computer match program against the Department of Motor Vehicle records of all fifty states and the District of Columbia. The abductor's car can then be located, even if it has a license plate from a different state. Information about a new driver's license can help to locate a parent who has kidnapped a child.

All fifty states have missing children clearinghouses that are connected through an Internet forum and network donated by Compuserve. The network is run by the staff of the National Center for Missing and Exploited Children. The state clearinghouses can communicate instantaneously and confidentially. Individual clearinghouses are usually run by state police, who handle phone calls and inquiries from the public as well as from government officials and others involved in a search.

The functions of individual state missing children clearinghouses vary, but they usually include public education and information; communication with parents, attorneys, law enforcement personnel, and government agencies; and assistance in the location and recovery of parentally abducted children. Many state clearinghouses serve as the contact in international abduction cases under the Hague Convention. The Federal Parent Locator Service searches for parents who are not paying child support as ordered.

Private agencies, such as those listed at the end of this book, may also provide information to help a left-behind parent find a child.

Schools are a prime source of information about missing children. All children under the age of sixteen are required by law in most states to attend school unless arrangements are made for home instruction. A detective can trace the school registrations and transfer procedures that follow a child from school to school to track a missing child.[10]

Credit card companies, insurance companies, libraries, magazine and newspaper subscription records, medical care providers, places of worship, and the postal service may all provide clues that will lead police and government workers to the location of a child who was taken by a noncustodial parent. These are just some of the legal means parents can use to locate a child who has been abducted by a family member.

Six

SOME OF THE MISSING COME HOME

"WELCOME HOME" MAY NOT ALWAYS BE THE GREETING a missing child hears on his or her return. Feelings at reunions depend on a number of things, such as the reason that a child was missing from the home, the length of the separation, the family situation before the episode, and the experiences of the child while he or she was gone.

Some children, like six-year-old Jennifer who was lost for two days in a large city and recovered by volunteers in the community, receive a welcome with ribbons and shouts of joy from family, neighbors, and others who have read about the incident.

A young child who has disappeared for a short time may not be aware that he or she is thought to be missing and thus may not be affected. However, a child lost in the woods for a day and rescued by search dogs may suffer many long-term emotional effects after the excitement of the incident wears off. Similarly, life might be significantly changed for a two-year-old who is left unsupervised and wanders down the road clad only in a diaper. After the discovery of other incidents of neglect, the parent at fault might be imprisoned, and the child might be placed in foster care.

AFTER A STRANGER ABDUCTION

When a child returns after a nonfamily abduction, whole communities may be involved. The national attention that a kidnapping in Belgium attracted made the return home a continuation of a very traumatic experience for two young girls. They were found alive in the kidnapper's basement, where both had been sexually abused. These crimes aroused strong public feelings against Marc Dutroux, the main suspect, and others believed to be involved in abducting and sexually abusing children. More than 300,000 people marched silently in protest through the streets of Brussels, Belgium, on October 20, 1996, to express outrage at the crime and the way it was handled by authorities. No one can fully realize the terror experienced by these victims during their ordeal or the emotional problems it may cause in the years to follow.[1]

Victims of stranger abductions often have recurring problems long after they return home. Law enforcement officers involved in the initial recovery of a missing child can provide some comfort and reassurance. They must also make decisions about the child's physical and emotional status.

A child who is recovering from a kidnapping may suffer from serious health problems, and these take priority over other less immediate problems. If Mel had been hidden in an abandoned building where he was chewed on by rats, denied food, and physically tortured, his parents would have to wait until doctors could examine him and administer treatment before welcoming him home. While they waited, law enforcement officers could try to prepare them by discussing the emotions Mel probably

In October, 1996, about 300,000 people dressed in white and carrying white flowers and balloons marched through central Brussels to support the families of victims of a man charged with abducting and murdering young girls.

experienced and guiding them in ways to deal with future emotional troubles. At the same time, arrangements could be made for a meeting of parents and child in a private location so that chaos and confusion would be kept to a minimum.[2]

AFTER A PARENTAL KIDNAPPING

A return home from a parental kidnapping may evoke a very different reunion from one greeting by a child returning from a stranger abduction—although, as with stranger kidnappings, each case is different. If a child wanted to leave the custodial parent and cooperated with the kidnapper, returning home could be an especially difficult time. In another situation, a child who thought a beloved parent was dead would be overjoyed to be reunited with that parent and angry with the kidnapper.

The parent who abducts a son or daughter may not be motivated solely by love and concern for the child. Sometimes, a parent is using the son or daughter as a pawn to seek revenge for a divorce, as a bargaining chip to reduce support obligations, or to force a reconciliation.

If the abducting father or mother has manipulated a child or forced him or her to make a choice between parents, the child may suffer before and after being returned to the parent who has legal custody. Imagine living with a devoted mother for seven years and then being snatched from the school grounds by the father you had not seen for a year. He treats you well but says that your mother does not want you any more, that she is marrying another man and has forbidden him to let you call her. This seems strange, but your father threatens to abandon you in the strange city to which you have moved if you try to contact her. The father you knew in the first six years of your life was a loving, caring person. You cannot believe he would lie to you, but you keep wondering how your mother could do such a thing.

For children in this kind of situation, sometimes the easiest solution is to accept what has happened and embrace the father as the closest parent again. By the time the mother finds the child, he or she may have developed strong emotional feelings for the father. Imagine learning that the mother you thought did not want you had been searching for you in every possible way. Now imagine your feelings upon discovering that the mother or father you had been told was dead was really alive but had been unable to find you.

In some cases of parental snatching, the abductor tires of caring for the child or never really wanted the responsibility. If he or she still wants to inflict pain on the searching parent, the child may be placed in foster care under another name or even put up for adoption through black-market methods.[3] Such a child may never come home. If he or she does, the honeymoon that follows the welcome home period may come to an end when house rules are put into action. The kidnapping parent may have imposed looser discipline than the custodial parent. Standards accepted by the child before abduction may seem unfair when compared with the laxness experienced during the time away from home. It may take years before a readjustment is made, or the return to normal family relationships may never happen.

Altering the name and appearance of a child is not uncommon in cases of parental abduction, and the number of times this is done can have an effect on the emotional growth of a boy or girl of almost any age. A short time away from home may be upsetting, but imagine how difficult it would be to return to a parent when there had been no contact over a period of years.

While some children adapt to change easily, others, especially those who are very shy, can become emotionally and physically ill from the pressure of trying to make new friends in strange classrooms. Even frequent changes in physical surroundings can make life difficult. A kidnapped child may find it difficult to trust new doctors and dentists, or health care may be neglected because a child is being hidden. These are just some of the variables that play a part in how a boy or girl reacts to returning home after a parental kidnapping.

STAYING AWAY FROM HOME

Unlike kidnapped children, many of those who are counted among the missing do not want to go home, are afraid to go home, or cannot go home. The runaways and the thrownaways who have been raped in their own beds, told that they are a financial burden, or made unwelcome because they are gay or pregnant may not want a reunion. One parent may be accepting, but the other may not want any contact with the son or daughter. Some runaways try returning home, but they leave again, time after time. These are the chronic runaways.

Seventeen-year-old Pammy disappeared from home a dozen times between the ages of ten and fifteen. When interviewed by researchers, she remembered being raped

A COUNSELOR AT CHILDREN OF THE NIGHT OFFERS HELP TO A YOUNG RUNAWAY.

and abused from the age of seven by her mother's lovers and then by her stepfather after her mother remarried. She experienced many beatings from her mother. One incident when she was five was serious enough to require a hospital visit. Her drunken mother, who was bathing her, hit her so hard with a soda bottle that the bottle broke. Pammy did not remember how her older brother explained the injury to doctors at the hospital, where knowledge of such abusive behavior might have led to an investigation and her placement in a foster home.

The first time she ran away, at age ten, she got up one morning as if to go to school and started walking. She did not have a plan, so she just walked and walked until she began to get frightened as night approached. She thought she might be kidnapped if she stayed out all night so she turned around and walked back to her house. She slept in her stepfather's van, which was parked in the driveway. She knew that she would be found in the morning. Later, she explained that she ran away because she wanted to "knock some sense into my parents."

Although her parents were glad to see Pammy when they found her in the van in the morning, they continued to mistreat her. She was repeatedly sexually abused by her stepfather and physically abused by both parents. Pammy ran away from home eleven more times. She felt that her parents stopped caring whether or not she ran away after the second time she did it.

While away from home, Pammy became involved in a number of delinquent activities, including prostitution at the age of twelve. She said she did these things because she wanted to get her parents' attention, not entirely because she needed the money.

When Pammy ran away the last time, her parents were drinking heavily and her two-month-old sister had been removed from the home because of neglect. Pammy said her parents were glad that she ran away again; they would have thrown her out anyway. She had no desire to return home.[4]

AN EXIT FROM PROSTITUTION

Many teens who are missing are working as juvenile prostitutes. The longer they live on the streets, the less chance they have of coming home again. Drugs, sexual exploitation, homelessness, crime, and suicide lie in wait for long-term runaways.[5]

The Paul and Lisa Program serves many missing children who become victims of life on the streets. It was started in 1980 by Frank Barnaba, a business executive who was trying to help a girl named Lisa leave her life as a prostitute in New Haven, Connecticut. She failed to show up for an appointment with him at a diner. He discovered that she had died of a drug overdose—perhaps accidental, or perhaps administered by her pimp because he was angry that she was leaving him. Mr. Barnaba hoped that this teenager's death could be used to help others. With funding from church and community sources, he began this outreach program, based in Westbrook, Connecticut.

Mr. Barnaba and his staff often join the police when they are searching for a missing child, after notification by the National Center for Missing and Exploited Children. In his attempts to reach young people who have been drawn into the sexual underground of prostitution and pornography, he is often exposed to dangerous situations.

When a girl agrees to enter the Paul and Lisa program, she is immediately taken to a safe house in the Northeast. If she is unable to return home, she then enters a transitional living program in foster care. She is counseled for six months to improve her self-confidence and receives help with her education and the development of job skills.

The Paul and Lisa Program has grown through the

years. It now works with boys as well as girls and educates thousands of students in New York, New Jersey, and Connecticut about the unglamorous life on the streets. In addition to these educational activities and the transitional housing programs for former prostitutes, it has also provided long-term care for runaways and other street kids from thirty-three states and six foreign countries.[6]

Some runaways who become prostitutes do go home again, but many prostitutes become addicted to drugs, contract AIDS or other diseases, or die before the age of thirty. No one will ever know how many children and teens have been prevented from running away or assisted in returning home by organizations such as the Paul and Lisa Program, Children of the Night in California, and Whisper in Minneapolis. For information about how to contact these programs, see pages 98 to 107.

RUNAWAY HOTLINES

While teens who call a runaway hotline may not want to go home, they may want their parents, or one parent, to know that they are safe. Missy was sent away from home by her father when she admitted that she was pregnant. She found shelter at a friend's house, but she would not call home for fear her father would answer the phone. She sent messages to her mother through a hotline, where information about her new life was held in confidence. She hoped that after her baby was born, there would be a chance for a reunion with her family.

Runaway hotlines may help runaways or thrownaways find refuge in a shelter, but there are only enough shelters to help a small percentage of those who need it. The shelters are home for a short period of time, usually just a few days. Unfortunately, there are not enough funds or shelters to fill the needs of all who would like to stay longer. So, many runaways find themselves back on the streets or returning to the homes they ran from, no matter how bad that option may seem to be.

BRINGING THE MISSING HOME

The number of missing children who are recovered has grown in recent years because of increased public awareness, improved search techniques, more police cooperation, and intensified efforts by organizations such as the National Center for Missing and Exploited Children and others, some of which are listed on pages 98 to 107. These organizations provide many services in addition to those already cited in this book, but two of the most important are education to prevent abduction and the initiation of searches immediately after an abduction has occurred.

Unfortunately, every hour, about one hundred children are reported missing in the United States.[7] Some eventually return home, some do not want to return home, and some, who might have wished to return, cannot, because they have been murdered.

SEVEN

DEATH AT THE HANDS OF STRANGERS AND PEERS

RELATIVELY FEW CHILDREN ARE ABDUCTED BY strangers, and about one in five of these stranger-abducted children is killed.[1] In every case of abduction, however, the possibility of homicide haunts the families of the missing children. Reports of the death of an abducted child evoke horror and anguish, and the public may respond with fears for their own children or for the girl or boy next door.

Some cases of homicide by strangers astound us. How could such crimes have been allowed to happen? Perhaps the killer was already recognized to be a dangerous person or had even been imprisoned for criminal acts. In one case, two young sisters, DeAnn Emerald Mu'min and Alicia Sybilla Jones, were killed by a man who had befriended them and their mother in a neighborhood park. Howard Steven Ault, a thirty-year-old convicted sex offender, abducted these two girls on their way home from school, sexually assaulted them, and then strangled them. Their bodies were found in the attic of the building in which he lived in Fort Lauderdale, Florida.

At the time of the girls' murder, Ault was under house arrest for an earlier sex crime. His probation officer had visited him just a few hours before he is believed to have abducted the sisters. He was on the state registry of sex offenders, and his name and address had appeared on the front page of a small local newspaper as an offender. Even though he was allowed to leave his house only for specific purposes—such as work, shopping, and psychiatric treatment—he managed to strike again.[2] His actions stunned the community, and hundreds of people grieved over society's failure to protect its children.

In New York City, Veronica Brunson ran away from home and spent a year walking the streets. During that time, six public and social service agencies had contact with her, and she served short periods of time in jail for prostitution. None of the agencies intervened or acted firmly enough to save her life. It ended when she was pushed, or fell, from the tenth-story window of a seedy Manhattan hotel. Veronica was eleven years old when she became a prostitute and twelve years old when she died.[3] Although this incident was unusual when it was reported more than a decade ago, today, very young prostitutes are common on the streets. They are popular with men who seek young girls who may be virgins and free of the virus that causes AIDS. No one knows how many die without media notice.

CHILD MURDERS IN THE NEWS

Some murder victims make headlines when the bodies are discovered in a plastic bag or turn up riddled with bullets, but many cases make little impression on jaded newspaper readers. Even compassionate citizens often feel that there is almost nothing that they can do to prevent the kidnapping of children.

The murder of six-year-old JonBenet Ramsey drew a

large amount of media attention, along with complaints that a crime of this sort no longer draws public concern unless it occurs in a family of wealth or prominent social position. JonBenet's body was found on December 26, 1996, in the basement of her Boulder, Colorado, home. She had been gagged and strangled. Pictures of this little girl, who was popular on the child beauty pageant circuit, were shown on national television again and again. While many viewers found something grotesque about such a young child wearing lipstick, eye makeup, and showgirl costumes, people everywhere expressed shock and sadness at her death.[4]

Taking Action after Tragedy

Some of these tragic cases do lead to positive action. The Polly Klass Foundation is an example. Twelve-year-old Polly Klass was hosting a slumber party in her home in Petaluma, California, on October 1, 1993. That night, Richard Allen Davis, a criminal who had spent sixteen years behind bars, entered her home and abducted her at knifepoint, leaving her two friends in the house where her mother and half-sister slept. Davis, high on drugs, may have sexually molested Polly before murdering her and burying her body in an empty lot in a town about fifty miles north of Petaluma. No one knows why he turned up at Polly's house, but he claimed that after kidnapping her, he killed her to avoid going back to prison.

The sad story of Polly Klass, who should have been safe in her own home, made headlines throughout the United States. Her father, Marc Klass, worked to bring the case to public attention, and he is credited with helping to insure that repeat criminals in California are imprisoned for a long time. He is active in the Marc Klass Foundation for Children. The Polly Klass Foundation plays an important role in the prevention of kidnapping by creating programs for schools, parents, and communities on issues related to child safety; developing and distributing fliers about missing children; and providing guidelines for the recovery of missing children.[5]

MEGAN'S LAW

The case of Megan Kanka, age seven, affected the public so strongly that it led to demands for a law that would let a community know when a sex offender moved into its midst. The law became known as Megan's Law.

When Megan left her home and crossed the street to look for a friend one evening in the summer of 1994, she and her parents were unaware that three convicted sex offenders lived in another house on the street. Police say that one of these men, Jesse Timmendequas, had served time for fondling and nearly strangling a seven-year-old girl. He is believed to have lured Megan into his house by promising to show her his new puppy. He then raped and strangled her, and discarded her body in a nearby park. He was found guilty of the crime in 1997.[6]

Some people believe that Megan's Law is unfair because, by publicizing the presence of convicted sex offenders, it continues to punish them after they have already served time for their crimes, and it interferes with their rehabilitation. However, others contend that there is little evidence that sex offenders can be cured, and protecting children must be paramount. The passage of Megan's Law led to a national debate over how to protect children from sexual predators.[7] Criminal records demonstrate that many of these people are repeat offenders.

SERIAL KILLERS

Serial killers are people who kill again and again. Sometimes, a series of murders is so shocking that it arouses a community, or even a whole country. As mentioned on page 52, atrocities in Belgium in 1996 spawned an angry national movement in support of family values and demands for reform. Reports highlighted the child sex-trade and the police mishandling of cases of sexual abuse and murder.

The main offender, Marc Dutroux, had a record of crimes dating back to 1989. In a police report compiled before information about his crimes was made public, a paid police informer told authorities that Dutroux was building cells in the basements of his houses to hold children that he planned to send abroad later. The informer claimed that he had been offered $2,500 for each child that he kidnapped.

If action had been taken to confine Dutroux earlier, the deaths of Melissa Russo and Julie Lejeune might have been avoided. The girls disappeared while on a walk near their homes. Their pictures appeared on thousands of missing children posters in 1995 and 1996. Their buried bodies were discovered after intensive searches of Dutroux's properties. Autopsies and other evidence indicated that they probably died of starvation in their cells in March 1996. No one knows how long it would have taken to find them if it had not been for a search for another missing girl, Laetitia Delhez, who had been traced to one of Dutroux's houses.

Fourteen-year-old Laetitia disappeared while walking home from a swimming pool one night in 1996. She was seen getting into a white van. The witness thought that this seemed strange and jotted down the license number of the van. This led police to Dutroux's house where an initial search turned up nothing.

After the police interrogated Dutroux for hours, he gave them information about Laetitia and another girl, Sabine Dardenne, whom he had abducted while she was riding her bicycle to school nearly three months earlier. These two girls were being held in a basement cell of one of his houses. Both had been sexually abused.

After searches of five of Dutroux's other houses, police uncovered a number of bodies, including one of an accomplice. They also found child porn videos, porn magazines, guns, and drugs. A number of other people were arrested in this case, including some police officers who were accused of shielding Dutroux.[8]

Serial killers are rare but often clever. They have been known to rove over long distances in their pursuit of victims, perhaps to avoid being caught. Some of these killers target a particular category of person, such as prostitutes, beautiful women, or children. Wayne Williams, for example, was convicted in Georgia for the slaying of a child and the possible murders of twenty-seven other children.[9]

CHILD MURDERS THROUGHOUT THE WORLD

Children meet death for a variety of reasons. In addition to the deaths of children used as prostitutes in sex rings in countries around the world, some young lives come to an early end in wartime or in countries where little is done to protect the lives of street children. Human rights groups charge that shopkeepers in high-crime urban districts in Brazil pay the police to kill children suspected of stealing. Over a thousand children, many of them runaways, were killed in Rio de Janeiro in one recent year.[10]

In many countries, abduction of children is common. Abductions and murder by strangers are relatively rare happenings in the United States and Canada. However, in the United States, murder involving children occurs far more often as the result of random and accidental gun violence than because of kidnappings.

HOW MANY MURDERS?

Criminal justice experts compile statistics on juvenile homicide because information is considered to be one of

AN EARLY MORNING SCENE IN RIO DE JANEIRO, WHERE
STREET CHILDREN SLEEP ON THE SIDEWALK AS A SHOPKEEPER
SWEEPS THE AREA.

the most important weapons against juvenile crimes. They
find that juveniles are murdered at the rate of about seven
each day in the United States. Recent increases in juvenile
deaths from violence stem largely from rising teen murders.[11] One in 610 children will be killed by a gun before
the age of twenty, often accidentally in the child's own
home.[12] Children ages twelve to nineteen are the most common victims of street gunfire, and two-thirds of the victim-
izers are other juveniles.[13]

Most juvenile homicide victims knew their attacker;
only 14 percent of juvenile homicide victims are killed by
strangers.[14]

African Americans make up 15 percent of the juvenile
population, yet among juvenile homicide victims, blacks have
outnumbered whites since 1988. Various explanations have
been offered for this. Most experts believe that one major

reason is poverty, but this is not the whole answer. Poor African Americans tend to live in ghettos, whereas poor whites tend to be scattered through more diverse neighborhoods. Unemployment, racial discrimination, drug and alcohol abuse, hopelessness and anger, and the increased number of children born to inexperienced teen mothers—many of whom lack adequate parenting skills and physical resources—are cited as additional explanations for the high homicide rate in black communities. Poor housing, nutrition, and health—including frequent head injuries that some experts believe may be responsible for violent behavior—are suggested as contributing factors as well.[15]

Many people believe that most white murder victims are killed by blacks, but government statistics show otherwise. Between 1980 and 1994, 93 percent of juvenile homicide victims were killed by persons of the same race.[16]

Until the teenage years, homicide rates are about equal for boys and girls. In older age groups, boys are the more likely victims. Juvenile homicides have increased most in large cities. Drive-by shootings account for a number of juvenile deaths.[17]

The climate of fear is so great in some areas that just the presence of a group of teenagers can make a shop owner fearful of trouble. In November 1996, five friends walked toward their homes after eating Thanksgiving dinner at the home of one boy's aunt. They stopped at a delicatessen for some snacks. An argument broke out when an employee at the counter accused some of the boys of not paying for a package of cookies. A shot rang out from another part of the store, killing one of the boys and wounding another. [18]

RISING LEVELS OF VIOLENCE

Some observers point to increased violence in many areas of life. Rising levels of violence in schools has led some to add security guards and, in some cases, metal detectors. The effects of violence on television and in films have been debated for years. Inner-city kids may grow up in an atmosphere of violence in their neighborhoods. Today, gangs and drug-related violence have reached the suburbs and rural areas. The recklessness and bravado that often accompany teenage behavior, combined with a lack of skill in settling disputes without physical force, transform conflicts that once might have resulted in bloody noses to shootings when guns are present. Recruits in the drug trade, who protect their territory with violence, and kids who are concerned with self-defense and status-seeking are likely to carry guns.[19]

Government statistics show that the number of murders of both male and female juveniles has increased dramatically in recent years. Tabloid headlines trumpet "Boy from Foster Home, 9, Is Shot on Way to School," "Girl Caught in Crossfire from Cocaine Dealers," "Thirteen-Year-Old Bleeds to Death on Sidewalk."

Although the deluge of such headlines tends to numb the public's outrage, even in a citiy like Los Angeles, where drive-by shootings have been fairly common, the killing of a small child can still spark action. Stephanie Kuhen, a toddler, was in a car that made a wrong turn late at night into a dead-end street that gang members considered to be their turf. Some members of the gang began to throw trash cans as the driver of the car tried to turn around. Then, without warning, shots rang out. One of them killed the little girl. This murder prompted the appointment of a gang "czar" to combat the wave of violence in the San Fernando Valley, which produced twenty-five gang-related killings in the summer of 1996.

Police estimate there are 150,000 gang members in poor sections of Los Angeles County. They attribute 80 percent of the violent crimes in a thirty-block area of South Central Los Angeles to gangs.[20] Residents of other parts of the city will tell visitors to avoid that area, but some kids live there. In South Central Los Angeles, Harlem, and other inner-city areas, many kids grow up in rat-infested bedrooms, attend dilapidated schools, and breathe air fouled by incinerator fumes. They grow up in families where drug abuse, including alcoholism, is common, and many teens meet death at an early age as a result of drugs, street violence, or stress.

Minneapolis, Minnesota, has an unusually high murder rate; one that, as in other cities, has been linked to crack cocaine.[21] With the decline of crack use, murder rates have declined, but they are still tragically high. Many civic leaders in Minneapolis are involved in programs, such as hotlines, drug counseling, and neighborhood watches, to help protect their children from drive-by shootings and other violence.

The risk of a child being murdered has increased all over the United States, but this growth has been the smallest in the South.[22]

TRAGEDY AT DUNBLANE

When groups of children are killed, shock and sadness reverberate far and wide. In Dunblane, Scotland, a man went on a rampage in March 1996, killing sixteen five- and six-year-olds and their teacher. Twelve others were wounded. The killer, an embittered loner and suspected pedophile, entered the front door of their school. He fired his handgun as he ran along the corridor, wounding two teachers. Then he burst into the gymnasium and killed the children. One child who escaped death was found under the bodies of two of his friends. He had been trying to drag them to safety. Citizens of Dunblane, all of Scotland, and people around the world felt outrage and grief for the terrible loss of life.[23]

Rare incidents such as the one at Dunblane come to the attention of large numbers of people, but many of the statistics about children living in areas where homicide is a common occurrence lack a human face. It is essential to recognize that many children exist in what can only be described as war zones.[24] When they live in a culture of drug abuse and gang violence, they too often become part of it.

Jed was working in a fast-food restaurant after school to help his mother pay the rent. He knew how hard she worked, and she was not well. He began selling drugs to earn more money and, since he knew his mother would not approve, put the money in the bank so that he would be able to go to college. He planned to tell her that he had been given a scholarship. Jed was very tired after long hours at school, working at the restaurant, and dealing on the street. He quit the fast-food job. Then he tried taking uppers to keep him going. Next, he tried downers to make his life more even. Before long he was a regular drug user, and the money he planned to save was being spent on his own habit.

Jed is just one of many casualties in areas where drugs are easily available and honest money is in short supply. Gangs often take the place of families, and violence at home breeds violence everywhere. The potential for violence varies from city to city, from situation to situation, and from individual to individual. Increased attempts to understand and prevent this violence may help to prevent some deaths.

EIGHT

DEATH BY ABUSE AND NEGLECT

ABUSE AND NEGLECT ARE AMONG THE MOST SERIOUS threats to the lives of infants and small children. In the United States, they account for more deaths than falls, choking on food, suffocation, drowning, residential fires, and motor vehicle accidents.[1] About two thousand children die from abuse or neglect in the United States each year. This is about five children every day—and it is a conservative estimate.[2] Some estimates put the number of children killed by parents and caregivers at five thousand a year. Homicide rates for children four years of age and under have hit a forty-year high.[3]

The killing of babies—infanticide—is not new. In a number of early civilizations, it was a common practice. Ancient Greeks placed ailing babies on hillsides to die, Eskimos customarily killed one of most sets of twins, and China has a long history of parents killing daughters. The killing of newborns by servant girls and poor unmarried mothers was not uncommon in England's past. In 1922, a law was passed in England charging mothers who killed babies who were under a year of age with manslaughter, a lesser charge than murder. The offenders were given psychiatric treatment and seldom served prison terms.[4]

Through the years, many countries have come to understand the act of infanticide as a tragic response to severe social, economic, or emotional stress. No one knows exactly how many overwhelmed mothers in the United States kill their newborn babies today. According to Justice Department statistics, an estimated 250 desperate girls and women are driven to kill their babies each year, but these crimes are difficult to track since many of the corpses are never found.[5]

Children die at the hands of parents and caregivers in many different ways. They are beaten, stabbed, scalded, forcibly suffocated, intoxicated, poisoned, shaken to death, starved, pushed into rivers, and choked. A report of the United States Advisory Board on Child Abuse and Neglect, *A Nation's Shame*, lists the names, ages, causes of death, dates of death, and location of children who have been killed by parents or caregivers over the period of about two years. Here are some of the cases in the list. Cynthia Shepeard was dropped two stories when she was ten days old. Two-month-old TeSean J. Bond was force-fed fatal amounts of Epsom salts and liquid antacids. Five-year-old Brittany Scott died from massive head injuries. A three-year-old anonymous toddler died after being severely beaten because he was afraid of the dark. One-and-one-half-year-old Felicia Brown was beaten to death with the heel of a shoe.

Over the last decade a number of highly publicized cases of fatal abuse and neglect have played a part in making the public aware of the need for better supervision of children at risk. In 1987, six-year-old Lisa Steinberg died after being beaten by her stepfather, Joel Steinberg, who had illegally adopted her. Heda Nussbaum, who lived in the family in the role of wife and mother, was also battered severely by Joel Steinberg. This man's life was thoroughly examined after the death of Lisa, and he was convicted of manslaughter and sent to prison.[6]

The Steinberg case drew additional attention, and horror, because the abuser was an attorney. The 1996 case of the murder of the baby of two affluent young college students shocked a nation that is often accused of paying little attention when a poor black fourteen-year-old leaves her newborn to die. The students, Amy Grossberg and Brian Peterson Jr., who had been lovers in high school, have been charged with putting their newborn into a dumpster.

Amy was attending the University of Delaware and Brian was a freshman at Gettysburg College when their baby was born. Their actions might have gone unnoticed if Amy had not fainted in her dorm room on November 12, 1996, leading to the discovery that she had given birth in a motel room in Newark, Delaware, the night before. The infant's father had been with her, but this was not a joyous event. Their newborn was found wrapped in a garbage bag in the motel dumpster. The medical examiner stated that the baby's skull had been fractured "due to blunt force and shaking."[7]

These young people may have been in love with each other, but they were not ready to be parents. The nation asked how they could have performed the act of which they have been accused. They were college students and should have known that counseling and other options—such as allowing the child to be adopted, or a legal abortion—were available.

Questions about their behavior may not fully be answered, but Dr. Phillip J. Resnick, a professor of psychiatry at Case Western Reserve Medical School, suggests that the killing of newborns is typically committed by young, isolated women who deny to themselves that they are pregnant. Girls like Amy Grossberg may be able to hide the changes in their figures by wearing loose clothing. Some women may not realize that they are pregnant early enough to have an abortion because they have irregular menstrual periods. Some, who are in denial, find themselves giving birth in stores, at high school proms, and in college dorms. When the trauma of the delivery and the cries of the newborn break through the walls of denial, these girls may panic. They stop their babies' cries in a variety of ways. The newborns may be drowned in toilets, stuffed in compactors or dresser drawers, or thrown out a window. Such a mother thinks of her child as an object to be gotten rid of rather than as a baby. In this state of panic, she does not connect her situation with pregnancy.[8]

DRUGS AND FATAL ABUSE

Drug abuse is behind many young abuse and neglect fatalities. Can you imagine a mother allowing her toddler or young child to starve to death? Although it is unusual, it does happen, and occasionally these cases receive media attention. For example, Carla Lockwood, a thirty-two-year-old mother, was arraigned on charges of killing her seventh child, four-year-old Nadine. Nadine's emaciated body was found in her crib by Carla's estranged husband.

Lockwood, a drug abuser, gave birth to her eighth baby in a hospital and then left the child without even naming it. Social workers placed the baby in a home soon after birth. Carla Lockwood had tested positive for drugs two years before Nadine had been born. At home, six of Carla Lockwood's children slept together on the same mattress in a rat-infested apartment where the refrigerator was padlocked. Nadine, the youngest, slept in a blanket-covered crib where she grew weaker and slowly starved to death.[9]

Nadine is one tragic example of children who "fall through the cracks" of a social welfare system that is supposed to protect them. The media coverage of cases such as Nadine Lockwood's helps to focus attention on the fact that drug addicts make terrible parents.

The death of another child whose mother was a drug abuser also drew national attention to the problem of drugs and child fatalities.[10] Six-year-old Elisa, or Alisa, Izquierdo, died in 1994. Elisa's mother believed that her daughter had been put under a spell which had to be beaten out of her. After months of sexual abuse and beatings, her mother hit her so hard that the child's head bounced against a concrete wall, causing internal bleeding in her brain and death. Her body was so cut and bruised that a child welfare worker who examined her after her death said that it was the worst case he had ever seen.[11]

A DELIBERATE KILLING

After Susan Smith strapped her two young sons into her car and sent it plunging into a lake where they drowned, her actions were the subject of many questions about fatal child abuse and neglect. How could she commit such an act? Why? Until that awful day, on October 25, 1994, Susan Smith had appeared to be a good mother who kept her children clean, fed, safe, and warm, and was never seen spanking them. Many experts tried to determine what caused her actions. While some suggested that she wanted to be free of children for the man she now loved, others felt that her own history played a major role. Her promiscuity was blamed on her need to feel loved. Sexual abuse by her stepfather when she was a child had left emotional scarring that was a destructive force in her life. She had continued a sexual relationship with him into adulthood.[12] This publicized story is an example of how complicated each case of fatal child abuse may be.

The cruel realization that parents and caregivers can kill their babies and young children is difficult to understand and difficult to face. Even professionals who make policies, direct programs, and deliver services to troubled families find these actions deeply disturbing.[13]

A COMMUNITY'S ANGUISH IS REFLECTED IN THIS
MEMORIAL FOR TWO YOUNG CHILDREN MURDERED
BY THEIR DISTRAUGHT MOTHER.

It has been estimated that 85 percent of childhood
deaths from abuse and neglect are systematically misidenti-
fied as accidental, disease related, or due to other causes.
The question of who harmed a child is often not asked
or answered and, in too many cases, perpetrators go unde-
tected and harm or kill other children.[14]

NINE

"NOT ONE MORE DEAD CHILD"

YOUNG PEOPLE ARE SHOWN TALKING ABOUT BEING killed or threatened by gunfire in a number of recent and riveting public service ads on television. These ads end with the theme "Not one more." Sometimes the endings are slightly different, but the message is the same: "Not one more lost life," "Not one more grieving family," "Not one more dead child."

These ads are one of the ongoing efforts to educate the public about child abuse and murder. In a survey of whether or not the ads are effective, many adults reported talking to their children about guns, joining a neighborhood crime prevention group, or volunteering with a youth group after they saw the ads.[1] The ads appear to have helped increase public awareness, but there is no way to measure their full effect.

DECREASING THE VIOLENCE

Many young people are looking for ways to decrease the violence in their world. They are recognizing that even indi-

AN ADVERTISING COUNCIL COMMERCIAL
AIMED AT SAVING CHILDREN FROM VIOLENT DEATH

rect exposure to homicide can lead to a number of emotional problems, including depression, anxiety, impaired ability to learn and achieve, and behavioral problems.[2]

How many children around the world suffer from problems that put them at high risk of developing into criminals? How many, as adults, will take the lives of one or more children? Can society help to prevent the conditions that foster murder? Many of America's children are undernourished, undertrained, and trail their peers in other nations in areas such as health care.[3]

How can child care centers, churches, child advocacy programs, and other organizations help to improve conditions for children and make their lives safer? No one has provided complete answers to these questions, but some progress is being made toward decreasing violence.

In some cities, enforcing statutes against graffiti, truancy, noise, and other "quality of life" crimes has helped to reduce the general crime rate. Expanded controls on handguns, new laws making it easier to combat gangs, and visits by teams of police and probation officers to the homes of youths on probation to insure that they abide by the terms of their probation are credited with helping to reduce juvenile homicide and other violent crimes.[4]

In several large cities, increased cooperation between police and communities, along with aggressive police action, is curtailing some gang violence. Criminologists credit the decline in crime in New York, Boston, San Francisco, Las Vegas, and many other cities to neighborhood police action, changing patterns of behavior among teenagers, and a decline in the crack cocaine market. A large number of young men who were drawn into the violent world of crack cocaine in the late 1980s have been imprisoned or killed, possibly contributing to the decrease in crime rates since 1991. Many young people who are fed up with violence are working in groups to help stop the killings.

VIOLENCE PREVENTION PROGRAMS

Experts call for the inclusion of violence prevention programs in primary and secondary schools so that young people can learn to handle their anger in less dangerous ways than they do today. The majority of all homicides are crimes of rage or passion that usually occur between family members, friends, or acquaintances.[5]

A SAMPLE AD CARD FROM THE "NOT ONE MORE" CAMPAIGN
TO STOP DEADLY VIOLENCE.

In addition to education about youth homicide, prevention strategies include improving conditions for the
poor, creating jobs, establishing school and community
enrichment programs, stabilizing family units, and more.
Gun control was found to be especially important. Com-
puter-aided research at Harvard University found that
three-quarters of juvenile killers and their victims had been
involved with gangs, and that the authorities could identify
the dealers who made large numbers of illegal gun sales to
young people. As a result, city official intensified their focus
on gangs and guns in crime prevention strategies.[6]

Everyone agrees that there are no simple solutions,
but an increasing number of people are working to achieve
changes in the basic causes of the whole Pandora's box of
social problems.

THE NEED FOR SAFE HOMES

At the top of the list of problems is the need for safe
homes. Abuse of very young children in their own homes
has reached the level of a public health crisis and is similar

in scope to the destruction of teenagers by street gunfire.[7]

Sometimes a single case is so terrible that it sparks major public action. Adam Mann's short life and brutal death was one of these. It became the subject of a 1991 documentary shown on public television, and it prompted Congress to recommend new action to protect children from abuse.[8]

Five-year-old Adam Mann was beaten to death by his stepfather, Rufus Chisholm, with the participation of his mother, Michelle Mann. Many social service professionals had missed a series of red flags that should have warned them that Adam was in serious danger. After his death, Adam's brother told social workers that the thrashing that killed Adam started after his stepfather caught him horsing around on the bed. Adam fled to the kitchen, where his mother told his stepfather that he had broken a house rule by eating some cake. This led to the most serious beating. Adam's mother did not try to stop it, and the child died later that day.

The beating that led to Adam's death was not the first abuse that he suffered. The autopsy revealed over one hundred injuries to his body. The cause of death was listed as a broken skull, broken ribs, and a split liver, but at one time or another, nearly every bone in his body had been broken. When Adam died, there was no food in his stomach, and the autopsy showed that Adam had had practically nothing to eat for a couple of days.[9]

After each notorious case of fatal child abuse or neglect, there is a call for child welfare agencies to be revamped. One technique that seems promising is the sending of helpers into homes to work with parents. Helpers teach overburdened parents how to cope with their problems, provide some respite, and give them a chance to put things in perspective. Helper programs are now being used in thirty-five states to some extent.[10]

Although social welfare agencies attempt to keep families together, many tragic cases show that this is sometimes dangerous. However, children who are removed from their families because they are being abused or neglected may then languish in inadequate foster care. Foster children often plead to return home, no matter how bad conditions were there. Deciding where children should live is a difficult task for harried social workers. They must make the best possible decisions about whether children should stay in foster care or return home to parents who have abused them. Experts say that some child welfare workers have let cases slide for years because they find it so hard to make decisions.[11]

Some kids get bounced from one foster family to another, and they may wait from five to eight years to be adopted. Many stay in foster care until they become adults. In some areas of the country, 30 percent of the children who are reunited with their families are later returned to foster care because of continued abuse.[12]

No one knows how many babies and young children die without capturing the attention of the public or the authorities whose job is to try to protect children at risk. One of the recommendations of the United States Advisory Board on Child Abuse and Neglect was to improve data collection about child abuse and neglect fatalities. Another recommendation was the formulation of a national policy to reduce such fatalities.[13]

Many communities have established better neighborhood support systems in an effort to prevent child abuse and neglect. And in most states, there are death review teams that scrutinize the deaths of young children. The teams include health, social service, and criminal justice professionals in a multiagency, confidential forum. They investigate the deaths and work to improve services and create prevention strategies.

The few cases that receive widespread media attention

are just the tip of the iceberg. Professionals in the field of child abuse and neglect hope that America will awaken to the national shame of child maltreatment-related fatalities and hope that Americans will be galvanized to act now to prevent future tragedies.[14]

WORKING TOGETHER

A national effort to protect the children who go missing and to prevent the murders of the young begins with each individual, with every person whose response to the problem is to work to increase awareness, educate others, change laws, and demand more help from authorities.

Much abuse is prevented or stopped by members of organizations such as the National Association for the Prevention of Child Abuse and Neglect. This group provides educational material for professionals in the field and for the public. The National Clearinghouse for Child Abuse and Neglect also plays a major role in prevention by supplying statistics and information about where to go for help, and coordinating efforts of those working in the field. But these and other organizations that speak for children need help.

Another major resource for the recovery of runaways, thrownaways, and otherwise missing children is the National Center for Missing and Exploited Children. Formed in 1984, this private, nonprofit organization works in cooperation with the U.S. government's Office of Juvenile Justice and Delinquency Prevention, and is funded in part through this office. It is a national clearinghouse for information on cases of abducted, runaway, or sexually exploited youth. One of its many functions is education, and it supplies experienced speakers on child safety issues and prevention strategies to schools and organizations interested in helping with the problem.

The plight of these children is drawing an increasing amount of attention. In 1996, the National Advertising

Council began sponsoring a ten-year program called "Whose Side Are You On?" that runs ads on television, the World Wide Web, radio, and in print media, focusing on kids in trouble. More than 350 organizations are now united as the Coalition for America's Children, and they have thousands of ways, big and small, in which volunteers can make a difference. Call 1-888-544-KIDS, or reach them one at www.kidscampaign.org.

On June 1, 1996, hundreds of thousands of Americans stood together for children at the Lincoln Memorial in Washington, D.C. This national day of commitment was endorsed by over three thousand community, state, and national organizations that believe that individually and

GROWING CONCERN ABOUT GOVERNMENT SUPPORT FOR CHILDREN'S WELFARE AND PROTECTION PROGRAMS LED TO A MASSIVE "STAND FOR CHILDREN" MARCH THROUGH WASHINGTON IN 1996.

together we can and must improve the quality of life for children. There are many ways to help children, and the program Stand for Children asks that each of us commit to doing one thing to help one child each day.[15] For example, Marge goes to a nearby elementary school and spends an hour with an individual child each day of the week. Sometimes she helps the same child all week with reading, some weeks she works with a different child each day. Andrew spends one hour each week at a community center, instructing small groups of children in computer use. There are many different ways a person can help. Ask about opportunities at your library, community center, Y, local shelter, religious facility, school, or any volunteer group.

In spite of the efforts of many individuals and organizations, abuse, kidnapping by strangers and noncustodial parents, and other crimes against children are still occurring in great numbers. Many more voices must be raised to support children now, before any more are missing or murdered.

NOTES

CHAPTER 1

1. Andrew O'Hagan, *The Missing* (New York: New Press, 1996), p. xix.
2. Office of Juvenile Justice and Delinquency Prevention, "Missing Children: Found Facts," *Juvenile Justice Bulletin* (Nov./Dec. 1990), pp. 1–2.
3. National Center for Missing and Exploited Children, *A Report to the Nation: Missing and Exploited Children, 1984–1994* (Arlington, Va.: National Center for Missing and Exploited Children, 1994) p. 5.
4. National Center for Missing and Exploited Children, *A Report*, p. 5.
5. National Office of Social Responsibility, *Change*, vol. 5, no. 3, (1982), p. 19.
6. U.S. Advisory Board on Child Abuse and Neglect, *A Nation's Shame: Fatal Child Abuse and Neglect in the United States* (Washington, D.C.: Dept. of Health and Human Services, 1995), p. vii.
7. *Ibid.*, p. xxiii.
8. *New York Times*, June 12, 1996.

CHAPTER 2

1. National Center for Missing and Exploited Children, "Fact Sheet on Non-Family Abductions," December 31, 1995.
2. Missing Children's Registry, *Canada's Missing Children* (Ottowa, Ont.: Missing Children's Registry), p. 4.
3. Kathryn M. Turman, *Recovery and Reunification of Missing Children: A Team Approach* (Arlington, Va.: National Center for Missing and Exploited Children, 1995), p. 2.
4. *Smithsonian Magazine*, Oct. 1995, p. 78.
5. Grolier Electronic Encyclopedia, s.v. "kidnapping."
6. Kenneth V. Lanning and Ann Wolbert Burgess, eds., *Child Molesters Who Abduct: Summary of the Case in Point Series* (Arlington, Va.: National Center for Missing and Exploited Children, 1995), p. 21.
7. *New York Times*, Nov. 1, 1996.
8. *New York Times*, July 31, 1996.
9. Gerald Hotaling and David Finklehor, *Sexual Exploitation of Missing Children* (Washington, D.C.: Office of Juvenile Justice and Delinquency Prevention, 1988), p. 31.
10. Stephen Steidel, ed., *Missing and Abducted Children: A Law Enforcement Guide* (Arlington, Va.: National Center for Missing and Exploited Children, 1994) pp. 49–50.
11. *New York Times*, Aug. 17, 1996.
12. "The Danger Years," *Life*, July 1995, pp. 40–45.
13. *New York Times*, Oct. 5, 1996.
14. *New York Times*, Nov. 16, 1996.
15. Martin L. Forst and Martha Elin Bloomquist, *Missing Children: Rhetoric and Reality* (New York: Lexington, 1991), pp. 85–86.
16. *Ibid.*, p. 86.
17. *Ibid.*, p. 58.
18. *Ibid.*, p. 59.

CHAPTER 3

1. *New York Times,* July 14, 1996.
2. *New York Times,* Sept. 27, 1996.
3. *U.S. News and World Report,* Mar. 20, 1996, pp. 71–72.
4. Geoffrey L. Greif and Rebecca L. Hegar, *When Parents Kidnap: The Families behind the Headlines* (New York: Free Press), p. 59.
5. *Ibid.,* p. 63.
6. *U.S. News and World Report,* Sept. 30, 1996, p. 26.
7. Greif, p. 141.
8. George Hotaling and David Finklehor, *Sexual Exploitation of Missing Children* (Washington, D.C.: Office of Juvenile Justice and Delinquency Prevention, 1988), p. 29.
9. *Summary from Additional Analysis of Data from the National Incidence Studies of Missing, Abducted and Thrownaway Children.* (Arlington, Va.: National Center for Missing and Exploited Children, 1997) p.1.
10. Greif, pp. 142–143.
11. Patricia Hoff, Judith Schretter, and Donna Aspell, *Family Abduction* (Arlington, Va.: National Center for Missing and Exploited Children, 1994) pp. 77–78.
12. Greif, p. 3.
13. National Center for Missing and Exploited Children, *A Report to the Nation* (Arlington, Va.: National Center for Missing and Exploited Children, 1994), p. 11.
14. Hoff, Schretter, and Aspell, *Family Abduction,* p. 59.
15. Greif, pp. 54–55.

CHAPTER 4

1. Office of Juvenile Justice and Delinquency Prevention, "Missing Children: Found Facts" (Washington, D.C.: Nov./Dec. 1990), p. 2.
2. Martin L. Forst and Martha Elin Bloomquist, *Missing*

Children: Rhetoric and Reality (New York: Lexington, 1991), p. 210.

3. National Center for Missing and Exploited Children, *A Report to the Nation* (Arlington, Va.: National Center for Missing and Exploited Children, 1994), p. 5.
4. David Finkelhor, Gerald Notaling, and Andrea Sedlak, *Missing, Abducted, Runaway and Thrownaway Children in America* (Washington, D.C.: Office of Juvenile Justice and Delinquency Prevention, 1990), p. xx.
5. Kathryn M. Turman, *Recovery and Reunification of Missing Children: A Team Approach* (Arlington, Va.: National Center for Missing and Exploited Children, 1995), p. 2.
6. Forst, pp. 192–193.
7. *Missing Children*, p. 3.
8. U.S. Attorney's Advisory Board on Missing Children, *America's Missing and Exploited Children* (Washington, D.C.: Office of Juvenile Justice and Delinquency Prevention, 1986), p. 7.
9. Turman, p. 187.
10. Forst, p. 187.
11. *Ibid.*, p. 188.
12. National Center for Missing and Exploited Children, *A Report*, p. 4.
13. U.S. Attorney's Advisory Board, *America's Missing*, p. 2.
14. Forst, p. 210.
15. Turman, p. 2.
16. *New York Times*, Aug. 17, 1996.
17. *New York Times*, July 13, 1996.

CHAPTER 5

1. National Center for Missing and Exploited Children, *A Report to the Nation* (Arlington, Va.: National Center for Missing and Exploited Children, 1994) p. 7.

2. Stephen Steidel, ed., *Missing and Abducted Children: A Law Enforcement Guide* (Arlington, Va.: National Center for Missing and Exploited Children, 1994), p. 27.
3. Michael Medaris, "The Missing and Exploited Children's Program," Office of Juvenile Justice and Delinquency Prevention, fact sheet no. 61, March 1997.
4. National Center for Missing and Exploited Children Website, www.missingkids.com
5. *Smithsonian Magazine*, Oct. 1995, p. 78.
6. C. Hatcher et. al., *Families of Missing Children* (Washington, D.C.: Office of Juvenile Justice and Delinquency Prevention, 1992), p. 1.
7. J. C. Paterson, *Investigator's Guide to Missing Children Cases* (Arlington, Va.: National Center for Missing and Exploited Children, 1987), pp. 33–34.
8. Marianne Takas and Deborah Bass, *Using Agency Records to Find Missing Children: A Guide for Law Enforcement* (Washington, D.C.: Office of Juvenile Justice and Delinquency Prevention, 1996), p. 1.
9. Kathryn M. Turman, *Recovery and Reunification of Missing Children: A Team Approach* (Arlington, Va.: National Center for Missing and Exploited Children, 1995), p. 17.
10. Takas, p. 4.

CHAPTER 6

1. *New York Times*, Nov. 4, 1996.
2. Kathryn M. Turman, *Recovery and Reunification of Missing Children: A Team Approach* (Arlington, Va.: National Center for Missing and Exploited Children, 1995), p. 13.
3. Mark-Davis Janus, et al., *Adolescent Runaways* (Lexington, Mass.: D. C. Health, 1987), p. 36.
4. *Ibid.*, pp. 36–39.
5. Office of Juvenile Justice and Delinquency Prevention,

"Missing Children: Found Facts," *Juvenile Justice Bulletin* (Nov./Dec. 1990), p. 2.
6. Paul and Lisa Program, flier and personal interview.
7. National Center for Missing and Exploited Children, *A Report to the Nation* (Arlington, Va.: National Center for Missing and Exploited Children, 1997) pp. 1–4.

CHAPTER 7

1. *Smithsonian Magazine*, Oct. 1995, p. 78.
2. *New York Times*, Nov. 13, 1996.
3. Clifford Lendecker, *Children in Chains* (New York: Everest House, 1981), p. 42.
4. *New York Times*, Jan. 10, 1997.
5. Polly Klass Foundation, 1996.
6. *New York Times*, June 1, 1997.
7. *Economist*, Oct. 19, 1996, p. 50.
8. *New York Times*, Aug. 22, 1996 and Nov. 4, 1996.
9. Margaret O. Hyde and Lawrence Hyde, *Missing Children* (New York: Franklin Watts, 1984), p. 45.
10. *New York Times*, Nov. 29, 1996.
11. *New York Times*, Aug. 6, 1996.
12. Children's Defense Fund, "Stand for Children," flier, 1996.
13. *Life*, "The Danger Years," July 1996, p. 50.
14. Howard N. Snyder and Melissa Sickmund, *Juvenile Offenders and Victims: A National Report* (Washington, D.C.: Office of Juvenile Justice and Delinquency Prevention, 1995), p. 23–26.
15. Paul C. Holinger et al., *Suicide and Homicide among Adolescents* (New York: Guilford, 1994), pp. 157–58.
16. Snyder, p. 24–25.
17. *Ibid.*, p. 25.
18. *New York Times*, Nov. 30, 1996.
19. Alfred Blumstein, "Violence by Young People," *National Institute of Justice Journal* (Aug. 1995), p. 6.

20. *Christian Science Monitor,* Sept. 25, 1996.
21. *New York Times,* June 30, 1996.
22. Snyder, p. 25.
23. *Newsweek,* March 25, 1996, p. 25–27.
24. Holinger, p. 177.

CHAPTER 8

1. U.S. Advisory Board on Child Abuse and Neglect, *A Nation's Shame: Fatal Child Abuse and Neglect in the United States* (Washington, D.C.: Dept. of Health and Human Services, 1995), p. xxv.
2. *Ibid.,* p. xxiii.
3. *Ibid.,* p. xxiv.
4. *New York Times,* Dec. 28, 1996.
5. *New York Times,* Dec. 22, 1996.
6. U.S. Advisory Board, *A Nation's Shame,* p. xxvi.
7. *Newsweek,* Dec. 2, 1996, pp. 92–94.
8. *New York Times,* Dec. 22, 1996.
9. *New York Times,* Sept. 2, 1996 and Sept. 30, 1996.
10. *New York Times,* Nov. 24, 1996.
11. *Time,* Dec. 11, 1996, p. 42.
12. *New York Times,* July 27, 1995.
13. U.S. Advisory Board, *A Nation's Shame,* pp. xv, xxix.
14. *Ibid.,* p. xxviii and xxix.

CHAPTER 9

1. Catalyst for Community Crime Prevention, "Survey Confirms Timeliness of 'Not One More' Ads" (Washington, D.C.: National Crime Prevention Council, 1996), pp. 5–6.
2. Paul C. Holinger et al., *Suicide and Homicide among Adolescents* (New York: Guilford, 1994), p. 176.
3. *Christian Science Monitor,* Mar. 4, 1997.
4. *New York Times,* Feb. 20, 1997.

5. Holinger, p. 155.
6. *New York Times*, Feb. 20, 1997.
7. U.S. Advisory Board on Child Abuse and Neglect, *A Nation's Shame: Fatal Child Abuse and Neglect in the United States* (Washington, D.C.: Dept. of Health and Human Services, 1995), p. xxiv.
8. *Ibid.*, p. xxiii.
9. *Ibid.*, p. xxiii.
10. *Life*, Sept, 1996, p. 58.
11. *New York Times*, July 27, 1994.
12. *Christian Science Monitor*, Dec. 23, 1996.
13. U. S. Advisory Board, *A Nation's Shame*, p. xxiii.
14. *Ibid.*, p. xxxvi.
15. Children's Defense Fund, "Stand for Children," flier, 1996.

FOR MORE INFORMATION

Artenstein, Jeffrey. *Runaways in Their Own Words*. New York: Tom Doherty Books, 1990.

Burgess, Ann W., and Kenneth V. Lanning. *An Analysis of Infant Abductions*. Arlington, Va: National Center for Missing and Exploited Children, 1995.

Crewdson, John. *By Silence Betrayed: Sexual Abuse of Children in America*. Boston: Little Brown, 1988.

Forst, Martin L. and Martha Elin Bloomquist. *Missing Children: Rhetoric and Reality*. New York: Lexington, 1991.

Girdner, Linda, and Patricia Hoff. *Obstacles to the Recovery and Return of Parentally Abducted Children*. Washington, D.C.: Office of Juvenile Justice and Delinquency Prevention, 1994.

Goldentyer, Debra. *Family Violence*. Austin: Raintree, 1995.

Greenberg, Keith E. *Runaways*. Minneapolis: Lerner, 1995.

Greif, Geoffrey L., and Rebecca L. Hegar. *When Parents Kidnap: The Families behind the Headlines*. New York: Free Press, 1993.

Hoff, Patricia, Judith Schretter, and Donna Aspell. *Family*

Abduction. Arlington, VA: National Center for Missing and Exploited Children, 1994.

Holinger, Paul C., et al.: *Suicide and Homicide among Adolescents.* New York: Guilford, 1994.

Hyde, Margaret O. *Kids In and Out of Trouble.* New York: Cobblehill, Dutton, 1995.

Hyde, Margaret O., and Elizabeth Forsyth. *Sexual Abuse of Children and Adolescents.* Brookfield, Conn: Millbrook, 1997.

Kozol, Jonathan. A*mazing Grace: The Lives of Children and the Conscience of a Nation.* New York: Crown, 1995.

Lanning, Kenneth V, and Ann Wolbert Burgess. *Child Molesters Who Abduct: Summary of the Case in Point Series.* Arlington, Va.: National Center for Missing and Exploited Children, 1995.

Missing Children's Registry. *Canada's Missing Children.* Annual Report. Ottowa, Ont.: Missing Children's Registry.

National Center for Missing and Exploited Children, *A Report to the Nation: Missing and Exploited Children, 1984–1994,* Arlington, Va.: National Center for Missing and Exploited Children, 1994.

Office of Children's Issues. *International Parental Child Abduction.* Washington, D.C.: U.S. Dept. of State, Bureau of Consular Affairs, 1995.

O'Hagan, Andrew. *The Missing.* New York: New Press, 1996.

Parent, Marc. *Turning Stones: My Days and Nights with Children at Risk.* New York: Harcourt Brace, 1996.

Steidel, Stephen, ed. *Missing and Abducted Children: A Law Enforcement Guide.* Arlington, Va.: National Center for Missing and Exploited Children, 1994.

Switzer, Ellen. *Anyplace but Here: Young, Alone, and Homeless—What to Do.* New York: Atheneum, 1992.

Takas, Marianne and Deborah Bass. *Using Agency Records to Find Missing Children: A Guide for Law Enforcement.*

Washington, D.C.: Office of Juvenile Justice and Delinquency Prevention, 1996.

Turman, Kathryn M. *Recovery and Reunification of Missing Children: A Team Approach.* Arlington, Va.: National Center for Missing and Exploited Children, 1995.

U.S. Advisory Board on Child Abuse and Neglect. *A Nation's Shame: Fatal Child Abuse and Neglect in the United States.* Washington, D.C.: Dept. of Health and Human Services, 1995.

ORGANIZATIONS CONCERNED WITH MISSING CHILDREN

The following organizations provide a wide variety of services for those searching for missing children and those who are working to keep children safe. Services vary, but include hotlines for sightings, assistance in searches and rescues, counseling, posters, prevention and education materials, legal help, and more.

The list, based on material from the National Center for Missing and Exploited Children, does not include all organizations and the information changes frequently.

NATIONAL

National Center for Missing and Exploited Children

(800) THE LOST
Website:
http://www.missingkids.com/

ARIZONA

The Nation's Missing Children's Organization, Inc.
12235 N. Cave Creek Road, Suite 6
Phoenix, AZ 85022

(602) 944-1768
E mail: nmco-aol@bham.net
FAX (602) 944-7520
Website: http://www.bham.net/

Our Town Family Center
3833 East 2nd Street
Tucson, AZ 85716

(602) 323-1708
FAX (602)323-5900

California

Amber Foundation for
Missing Children
2550 Appian Way,
#204/P. 0. Box 565
Pinole, CA 94564

(800) 541-0777
FAX (510) 758-0319

Child Quest International, Inc.
1625 The Alameda, Suite 400
San Jose, CA 95126
(sightings only)

(408) 287-HOPE
(800) 248-8020
FAX (408) 287-4676
E-mail: info@kids.org
Website: http://www.kids.org/

Children of the Night
14530 Sylvan Street
Van Nuys, CA 91441

(818) 908-4474
FAX (818) 908-1468

Find the Children
11811 W. Olympic Boulevard
Los Angeles, CA 90064

(310) 477-6721
FAX (310) 477-7166
E-mail:
76042.3172@compuserve.com

Interstate Association for
Stolen Children
10033 Yukon River Way
Rancho Cordova, CA
95670-2725

(916) 631-7631
FAX (916) 631-1009
E-mail:iasckids@packbell.net

The Polly Klaas Foundation
P.O. Box 800
Petaluma, CA 94953

(707) 769-4055
(800) 587-4357
FAX (707) 769-4019
Website: http://www.pklaas.com/

Vanished Children's Alliance
2095 Park Avenue
San Jose, CA 95126

(408) 296-1113
(800) 826-4743 (for sightings)
FAX (408) 296-1117
Website:
http://www.fga.com/vanished/

CONNECTICUT

The Paul and Lisa Program (860) 767-7660
P.O. Box 348 FAX (860) 767-3122
Westbrook, CT 06498

FLORIDA

Child Watch of North America, Inc. (407) 363-9313
7380 Sand Lake Road, Suite 500 (800) 928-2445
Orlando, FL 32819 FAX (407) 290-1613

International Center for the Search (407) 382-7762
and Recovery of Missing Children (800) 887-7762
5456 Hoffner Avenue, Suite 204 FAX (407) 382-8673
Orlando, FL 32812 E-mail: johnnyr@ao.net

Missing Children Center, Inc. (407) 327-4403
276 East Highway 434 FAX (407) 327-4514
Winter Springs, FL 32708

Missing Children Help Center (813) 623-5437
410 Ware Boulevard, Suite 400 (800) USA-KIDS
Tampa, FL 33619 FAX (813) 664-0705
E-mail: 800usakids@compuserve.com
Website: http://www.800usakids.org/

GEORGIA

Children's Rights of America, Inc. (770) 998-6698
8735 Dunwoody Place, Suite 6 (800) 442-HOPE
Atlanta, GA 30350 FAX (770) 998-3405

IOWA

Iowa's Missing and Exploited (712) 252-5000
Children, Inc. FAX (712) 258-2756
Terra Centre, Suite 129
Sioux City, Iowa 51101

KENTUCKY

Exploited Children's Help
Organization
2440 Grinstead Drive
Louisville, KY 40204-2304

(502) 458-9997
FAX (502) 458-9797

MARYLAND

Missing and Exploited Children's
Association
P.O. Box 608
Lutherville, MD 21094

(410) 667-0718
(410) 282-0437

MINNESOTA

Jacob Wetterling Foundation
P.O. Box 639
St. Joseph, MN 56374

(320) 363-0470
(800) 325-HOPE
FAX (320) 363-0473
E-mail: jacob@uslink.net
Website: http://www.jwf.org/

Missing Children—Minnesota
P.O. Box 11216
Minneapolis, MN 55411

(612) 521-1188
(888) RUN-YELL

MISSOURI

Lost Child Network
7701 State Line Road, Suite B
Kansas City, Mo 64114

(816) 361-4554
FAX (800) 729-3463
E-mail: lostchildnet@uno.com

NEVADA

Nevada Child Seekers
25 TV5 Drive
Henderson, NV 89014

(702) 458-7009
FAX (702) 451-4220

New Jersey

Services for the Missing, Inc.   (609) 783-3101
P.O. Box 26   FAX (609) 783-9442
Gibbsboro, NJ 08026

New Mexico

I.D. Resource Center of Albuquerque (505) 883-0983
2913 San Mateo, NE   FAX (505) 880-0948
Albuquerque, NM 87110

New York

Child Find© of America, Inc.   (914) 255-1848
P.O. Box 277   (800)A-WAY-OUT
243 Main Street   (800)I-AM-LOST
New Paltz, NY 12561-0277   FAX (914) 255-5706

AFFILIATES:
Friends of Child Find:
Montana: (406) 259-6999
Pennsylvania: (412) 241-1234

Oregon

National Missing Children's   (503) 257-1308
Locate Center   (800) 999-7846 (for sightings)
P.O. Box 20007   FAX (503) 257-1443
Portland, OR 97220   E-mail:nmclc@cybernw.com

AFFILIATE:
Affiliate: National Missing   (613) 729-7678
Children's Locate Centre   Website:
(Canada)   http://www.cybernw.com/~nmclc/

National Missing Children's   (615) 504-KIDS
Locate Center (Tennessee)   (615) 504-5437
International Hotline   (800) 999-7846
(serves USA, Canada, and
South America)

PENNSYLVANIA

Children's Rights of   (610) 437-2971
Pennsylvania, Inc.   FAX (610) 437-4090
P.O. Box 4362
Allentown, PA 18105

RHODE ISLAND

The Society for Young Victims   (401) 353-9000
1920 Mineral Spring Avenue,   (800) 999-9024
Suite 16   FAX (401) 353-9001
North Providence, RI 02904

TENNESSEE

Commission on Missing and   (901) 528-8441
Exploited Children (COMEC)   FAX (901)575-8839
Juvenile Court
616 Adams Avenue, Room 102
Memphis, TN 38105

TEXAS

Child Search   (281)537-2111
National Missing Children Center (800) 832-3773
P.O. Box 73725   FAX (713) 355-6477
Houston, TX 77273-3725   Website: http://www.childsearch.org/

Heidi Search Center, Inc.
7900 North IH 35
San Antonio, TX 78218

(210) 650-0428
FAX (210) 650-3653
Website:
http://www.halcyon.com/alt.
missing-kids.gifs/HSC.html

WASHINGTON

Operation Lookout/National
Center for Missing Youth
6320 Evergreen Way
Everett, WA 98203

(425) 771-7335
(800) LOOKOUT, ext. 1234
FAX (425) 348-4411
E-mail:lookout@premierl.net
Website:
http://www.premierl.net/~lookout/

WISCONSIN

Youth Educated in Safety, Inc.
P.O. Box 3124
Appleton, WI 54915

(920) 734-5335
(800) 272-7715
FAX (920) 734-7077

CANADA

Child Find Canada
710 Dorval Dr., Suite 404
Oakville, Ontario
Canada L6K 3V7

(905) 845-3463
(800) 387-7962
Toll free number serves Canada
and USA
FAX (905) 845-9621

PROVINCIAL OFFICES

Alberta
(403) 270-3463
FAX: (403) 270-8355

Edmonton
(403) 465-1003
FAX: (403) 463-1136

British Columbia
(604) 251-FIND
FAX (604) 255-9968
Kelowna
(604) 763-2022
FAX: (604) 860-0843

Manitoba
(204) 945-5735
FAX: (204) 948-2461

New Brunswick
(506) 459-7250
FAX: (506) 459-8742

Newfoundland
(709) 738-4400
FAX: (709) 738-0550

Ontario
(905) 842-5353
FAX: (905) 842-5383

Prince Edward Island
(902) 368-1678
FAX: (902)368-1389

Saskatchewan
(306) 955-0070
FAX: (306) 373-1311

Missing Children Society
of Canada
219, 3501-23 Street, NE
Calgary, Alberta,
Canada T2E 6V8

(403) 291-0705
(800) 661-6160
FAX (403) 291-9728
E-mail:
74737.132@compuserve.com
Website:
http://www.maracomm.com/ccsc/rncsc

The Missing Children's Network/
Le Reseau Enfants Retour Canada
231 St. Jacques, Suite 406
Montreal, Quebec
Canada H2Y 1M6

(514) 843-4333
FAX (514) 843-8211
E-Mail:missing@InterLink.NET
Website:
http://www.alliance9000.com/E/MCNC/11.
html and http://www.maracomm.
com/CCSC/MCNC/

North American Missing
Children Organization
Suite 205, Cambridge 2
202 Brownlow Avenue
Dartmouth, Nova Scotia
Canada B3B lT5

(902) 468-2524
FAX (902) 468-2803

HOTLINES

Check your phone book for local hotlines and support groups.

1-800-Cocaine

Alcoholics Anonymous
Al-Anon/Alateen
See the white pages of your phone book.

Boys Town National Hotline
1-800-448-3000

Childhelp USA (child abuse and domestic violence)
1-800-422-4453

National AIDS Hotline (CDC)
1-800-342-AIDS

National Center for Missing and Exploited Children
1-800-THE-LOST

National Child Abuse Hotline
1-800-4-A-CHILD
1-800-422-4453

National Institute on Drug Abuse/Helpline
1-800-662-HELP

National Runaway Hotline
1-800-HIT-HOME

National Runaway Switchboard/Youth Suicide Hotline
1-800-621-4000

National STD Hotline
1-800-227-8922

National Youth Crisis Hotline
1-800-448-4663

Nine-Line of Covenant House
1-800-999-9999

Our Missing Children (Canada)
1-800-843-5678 (toll free in North America)

SAMPLE MISSING CHILD FLIER/POSTER

Have You Seen This Child?

Wanted:
Arrest Warrant
Issued

Missing Child

OPTIONAL PHOTO OF ABDUCTOR (if warrant issued for arrest)	CHILD'S PHOTO	CHILD'S PHOTO DIFFERENT ANGLE
(Date of Photo)	(Date of Photo)	(Date of Photo)

NAME OF ABDUCTOR: NAME OF CHILD:

Date of Birth: Date of Birth: Age: Race:

Ht.:   Wt.:   Grade in School:

Hair: Eyes: Ht.:   Wt.:   Hair: Eyes:

Complexion: Complexion:

Scars, etc.:   Scars, etc.:

Occupation: Hobbies, sports, etc.:

Race: Details of Abduction—Date, Place:
                                              Indicate violation of court order, warrant
                                              on file. Indicate if abuse has occurred.

IF YOU HAVE ANY INFORMATION, PLEASE CONTACT:
Officer's Name, Police Department:
Telephone Number:
Case Number:
Warrant Number (if secured):

National Center for   1-800-THE-LOST
Missing and Exploited Children   (1-800-843-5678)

NOTE: A missing child MUST be registered with the National Center for Missing and
Exploited Children before adding NCMEC's name and telephone number to this flier.

INDEX